REVENGE OF THE SPANISH PRINCESS

Cornwall, 1695. When her beloved father dies with the name Lovett on his lips, privateer captain Catherina Trelawny vows revenge on the mysterious pirate. Seeking him on the Mediterranean island of Azul, she is charmed by the personable Henry Darley. But Cate finds her plan goes awry when Darley and Lovett turn out to be the same man. Cate and Henry set sail across the high seas battling terrifying storms, deadly shipwreck, dissolute corsairs — and each other.

LINDA TYLER

REVENGE OF THE SPANISH PRINCESS

Complete and Unabridged

LINFORD
Leicester

First published in Great Britain in 2020

First Linford Edition
published 2021

A catalogue record for this book is available
from the British Library.

ISBN 978–1–4448–4724–6

Published by
Ulverscroft Limited
Anstey, Leicestershire

Printed and bound in Great Britain by
TJ Books Ltd., Padstow, Cornwall

This book is printed on acid-free paper

1

1695

No matter which way she turned, Catherina Trelawny could not deny her altered appearance. She stood at the tall looking glass, shafts of sunlight filtering through the open portholes of the Spanish Princess and into her cabin. These months at sea had turned her womanly figure into a slim, almost boyish one. Wearing the practical clothing of a loose white shirt and dark breeches added to the impression, as did her tanned skin and mass of black wind-tangled curls tied back with a ribbon in the style of most sailors.

Cate chided herself. What did her appearance matter? She was not a foolish young woman with nothing on her mind but marriage. Since the death of her beloved father six months ago, she had proved herself the capable and proud captain of a privateer ship. She was young and still learning, but the men's regard for her father had helped her command the crew of twenty men and her own skill had maintained that respect.

It had been less easy to get her father's letter of authority from His Majesty, William III, made out in her name instead of his. She would not forget the curt reply when she'd pointed out to the Crown official that, although few, there were other female captains.

'Those women were pirates, madam, and therefore not acting under Royal authority.'

But Cate was determined and persuasive.

She glanced over at the small safe where she kept her letter of marque and smiled with satisfaction. The licence not only protected her and her men from being treated as pirates if captured by the Royal Navy, but also gave permission to loot merchant ships flying the colours of Britain's enemies. The War of the Grand Alliance meant that Britain's present foe was France.

The Spanish Princess slipped over the Mediterranean, towards her home in Cornwall. It had been a successful voyage, but it was time to return to Pentreath Castle. To wearing a pretty gown, having her hair dressed by a lady's maid and drinking tea out of a china cup. Almost without thinking, Cate lifted her tousled curls, coiled them on top of her head and pouted into the mirror.

'Very pretty, ma'am.'

Cate whirled round, dropping her hand, her hair falling down her back. 'Knock before you enter my cabin, Mr Morgan!'

'Beg pardon, Captain.' Her chief mate grinned as he stood in the low doorway, his short, stocky frame almost filling it.

'You may have served my father for many years, and known me since I was a little girl, but such behaviour is not excusable, Mr Morgan.' She placed her hands on her hips in an attitude of arrogance, but she could not be cross with him for long. 'Well, what is it you want?'

He stepped into the cabin. 'The look-out reports a ship on the horizon, ma'am. A sloop.'

She dropped her hands. 'Whose colours?'

'None flying.'

'It seems our adventures are not yet over for this voyage.' Plucking her jacket from the back of the chair, she pulled it on. 'Come.'

She sprang up the ladder and onto the deck, and Mr Morgan followed. The other ship was under full sail on the horizon. Cate drew the spyglass from her pocket and raised it to her eye. As she focused on the ship through the glass and tried to make out its origin, the vessel slowly began to change course.

'She's making directly for us, ma'am,' called the look-out.

'Very well,' said Cate. 'Mr Morgan, raise the colours!'

No sooner had this order been carried out, than the other sloop hoisted its own flag in reply.

'The jolie rouge!'

The flag was the red of pirates, but

emblazoned in the centre was a black initial.

Morgan said sharply, 'She's headed for our starboard side.'

'Prepare the men,' she commanded.

'Clear the decks for action!' he shouted. 'Gunners in position!'

As the crew ran to their posts, Cate saw their opponent was crossing towards them at speed. Spaced along the deck, the muzzles of their cannons gleamed and wisps of smoke drifted from long sticks held by the pirates.

She knew what to do. Her father had taught her well, yet her confidence faltered. This would be her first battle as captain. The French ships encountered in the voyage had put up only minor resistance before surrendering, as merchant vessels usually did. They valued their lives more than their cargo. She didn't blame them.

Cate turned to her chief mate.

'Their cannoneers are at their posts, ready to light the fuses. Who is this insolent captain?'

5

'Not known to me, ma'am,' said Morgan.

'Well, we'll soon have him in our range.'

The two sloops had drawn closer and she could see the black initial on the enemy's flag, but could not quite decipher what it was. The script was an elegant flourish, an S or an L. It meant nothing to her.

She dropped the spyglass into her pocket and took the speaking-trumpet Morgan handed her. Raising it, she shouted orders to her men. 'Come about to face the enemy! Starboard guns in position. Fire the cannons when I give the order.' She waited, watching the progress of their opponent and holding her nerve. Nearly there ...

'Fire!' she yelled.

The Spanish Princess's three cannons discharged their loads. The vibrations shook through Cate's bones. Her ears rang with the booms and the smell of powder tickled her nostrils and stung her eyes. When the smoke cleared, she could see the other ship had not been hit.

Morgan swore. 'Let's hope we reload in time.'

Their adversary changed course, making an arc to avoid being the target of the Spanish Princess's cannons. It moved swiftly, with all its sails set.

'He's going to double back and try to sink us.' Cate's heart quickened. She raised the speaking-trumpet. 'Get ready to face him.'

She waited as her ship swung round.

'Now he'll have to sail against the wind to get at our side,' said Morgan.

The other sloop adjusted course to intercept the Spanish Princess's new manoeuvre as Cate had expected. It flew over the waves, then stopped and turned into the wind.

'Clever.' Cate could not help but laugh. 'Pity he's our foe.' She turned to Morgan. 'Have the cannoneers reloaded?'

'Aye, Cap'n.'

'Fire when I give the order.' But before she could act, the enemy vessel fired.

Debris soared into the air around her and a deafening explosion echoed from side to side. The sky tilted as she was thrown upwards. She hit the deck flat on her back, felt a dull ache in her body as the air was forced from her lungs. For a moment she lay there, certain she had lost the battle. No, she thought, do not give in so easily. Panting, she pulled herself up and clung to the rail as her ship slowly righted itself. Her hair had come loose of its ribbon and the curls whipped around her face.

Morgan gained his feet and was heading to check the damage. The enemy's white sails flapped in the wind, closer now to the Spanish Princess. Through the smoke she could see the varnished wood of the other ship's hull as it glistened in the sunlight. Standing on its deck was a row of musket-armed men.

On the prow stood a tall, slim man, his black, full-skirted coat open and billowing in the breeze. A large black hat, trimmed with a long red feather and tilted low over his forehead, cast his face into shadow and obscured his features. The man's spyglass was trained on her and she frowned.

Musket shots rained on deck and she sprang back into action. 'Aim your guns at their bowsprit!' she shouted.

A hail of shot flew into the air. One cannon ball hit the enemy's bowsprit and split the wood with a thunderous crack. Its sail collapsed with a thud to the deck and a cheer went up from her men. They had won!

Her crew scrambled about on deck, picking their way between the debris, checking on damage and ship mates.

'We don't seem to be shipping water, Captain,' said Morgan.

'Very good, Mr Morgan.' Cate prayed there were no serious casualties among her crew and silently thanked her father for watching over them.

A movement on the other ship caught her eye. The figure in black standing on the prow. Silhouetted against the blue Mediterranean sky, he lowered his spyglass and raised his hand in a salute to the victor. She pulled her own spyglass from her pocket and put it to her eye. In the glass she saw his shadowy lips curl in a smile. Cate laughed and raised her hand in acknowledgement.

She hesitated to give the order to board and in that moment knew she would not do it. There was something about the pirate captain — she could not say what — that made her unwilling to push her advantage. Instead of leading her men to board the defeated ship and claim their spoils, she found herself giving the order to head for the open sea.

'Cap'n?' said Morgan, frowning. 'Shouldn't we be — ?'

'Not this time, Mr Morgan,' she said firmly.

As the Spanish Princess parted the waves, Cate looked back. The tall, black-coated figure removed his hat and executed a flamboyant bow.

★   ★   ★

Henry Darley, fifth Earl of Lovett, stood on the prow of the Oceanus, a wry smile on his lips. For the first time in his pirating life he had not only been bested by another sloop, but by one with a captain who was undoubtedly female. Her figure may have been slight, but through his spyglass he detected tell-tale curves as the breeze softly blew her shirt against her body. A remarkable woman. The ladies of his acquaintance in Dorset were foolish, simpering things.

'We need a harbour for repairs, sir.'

Henry turned to his chief mate and nodded.

'I'll speak to the carpenter to see if we can make it to Azul. Meanwhile, Mr Elphick, give the order to sail there.'

He crossed the deck to survey the damage to his ship and injuries to his pirate crew. The ship's doctor tended to a man with blood oozing from a gash in his thigh and Henry stopped to speak to both men. He walked on and crouched down next to an injured man slumped on a coil of rope. A bloody wound in his shoulder showed where a musket bullet had lodged itself.

Henry folded his clean linen handkerchief into a pad, gently pressed it onto the young man's wound and smiled reassuringly at him. 'The doctor won't be long, Thomas.'

'Aye, Cap'n.' The young man gave a faint smile.

Henry moved on. Another man lay with a jagged piece of shrapnel buried in his chest, his open eyes blank. Henry closed the man's eyelids and made the sign of the cross. He beckoned one of his uninjured men to fetch the dead man's hammock, and needle and thread.

Henry gave a sigh as he searched the dead man's pockets. He disliked doing this for it seemed disrespectful, but most of the men carried some small thing of sentimental value and Henry would return it to the man's family. In Felix's pocket he found a gold signet ring with a black stone and slid it into his own pocket for safe keeping.

'Sew Felix into his hammock,' he said, when the man reappeared. 'We will bury him shortly.'

The sun was low in the sky and the room growing dark as Henry entered his cabin. He removed his large-brimmed hat, dropped it onto the table and flicked the long feather with one finger. Untying his black bandana, he threw it after the hat and lifted his arms to light the lamp. The shadows swayed with the movement of the ship. He turned from the lamp, catching a glimpse of himself in his mottled shaving glass. The reflection showed a man with strong features and fair hair tied in the nape of his neck. Gentleman or pirate? Both, thought Henry, with a shrug.

When a child in Dorset, he had wanted nothing more than to join the Royal Navy and his father had given his blessing. Then Henry's elder brother died suddenly. Henry's grieving, widowed father withdrew his consent, desperate to keep safe his sole surviving child and heir. But for Henry the call of the sea was strong. To his shame, he'd left Melbury, joined the Navy as a junior officer and served his apprenticeship.

A few years later, his father passed away. Now a young man, Henry returned home, distressed by the pain he'd inflicted on his father and for not being by his bedside at the end. He threw himself into managing his father's estates and did this willingly and well. But he soon became restless to return to the sea.

Henry had seen the brutality of life in the King's Navy. He vowed to fit out his own ship and do things differently. It was easy for him to decide on the form of his new sea-faring life. Britain's trade with the east was increasing, other countries were involved in the race to expand their empires and pirates were gathering a share of the riches.

For part of the year, he was the respectable Earl of Lovett, running his estate in the southwest of England. But for the rest of the year he was pirate Captain Lovett, revelling in the thrill of life on the high seas.

Henry had no grudge against society and was not interested in bloodshed. What fascinated him was the organisation required to outwit the enemy, the excitement and the winning. But Henry never forgot that he was a gentleman. He treated his crew with courtesy. Whenever he secured the surrender of a captain and boarded the ship to find it contained a lady, he would beg her pardon, assist her back into her cabin and order his men to loot only the merchant's goods. Yes, he was both gentleman and pirate.

Henry threw himself into his chair, poured a glass of claret and reached for the navigation charts spread on the oak table in the centre of the cabin. The uppermost map showed the Mediterranean and he pulled it towards him. His finger tapped on the small island of Azul. Pirates were welcome there and safe from arrest. There were no men in blue uniforms strutting about with swords at their sides. They would stop at Azul for repairs and much-needed provisions. They would be there in two days if the temporary repair held and the wind continued in this direction.

His eye caught the edge of another chart. The English Channel. He pulled it out from under the map of the Mediterranean and looked at the familiar coastline of the south-west of England. He had not been home for some months. There was no one to miss him. Those acquaintances once interested in his life had become used to his being away at sea, first in the Navy and then when he let it be known he travelled in search of new experiences to occupy his mind. His man of business could be trusted to deal with the work of the estate. But there was something he could not quite identify. He was six and twenty years old, and living the life he'd always dreamed of, yet something was missing.

Henry gazed out of the porthole at the darkening sea. Once repairs were complete, the Oceanus would return to England. With a plunder of silks and jewels, it had been a profitable and satisfying voyage. Satisfying, that is, with the exception of the recent skirmish.

An image came to him of the young woman, her long raven curls blowing in the breeze, laughing as she lifted her hand to him. He smiled at the memory and felt his heart lift a little.

Cate stood at the wheel, feeling the wind on her back and the surge of the ship as the vessel swept forward. The sails hummed. Her heart thudded with the excitement of her first battle — and she had scored a victory over a mysterious enemy. Mr Morgan had still to inform her of any injuries to the men and the exact damage to the ship, but they were sailing without any obvious problems, which bode well. Her head ached a little and her back felt bruised from being thrown to the deck, but her spirits were high.

Morgan reappeared by her side.

'What do you have to report, Mr Morgan?'

'A wound to Peter Davies's leg and a piece of shrapnel in the hand of Robert the cabin boy. The injuries are being dealt with. There's some damage to the deck, but we can get that repaired at our next port.'

'Thank you, Mr Morgan. We'll make

for Azul. That's the nearest safe harbour.'

'Aye, Cap'n. If conditions continue as they are, we should be there in two or three days. Perhaps we could stay on the island for a bit? The men would like some recuperation.'

'Women and drink, you mean.' The crew expected this at every port and it would be pointless to try to change things. She nodded, then called the helmsman to take the wheel and said to Morgan, 'I'll speak to Peter and young Robert, then I'll be in my cabin if you need me.'

When she had satisfied herself the two men would be well, Cate stepped down into her quarters. An oil lamp swung gently from the overhead of the cabin and she reached up to light it. Night had not yet fallen, but darkness was gathering below deck. The lantern flared into life and settled to cast shadows in the corners of the cabin. She stretched out on the low divan and idly listened to the men shouting and singing as they worked on deck above.

Cate wondered what her mother would think of her life now. Gabriela, the daughter of a wealthy Spanish merchant, had been sailing to Malta to meet a much older man her father wished her to marry. The ship was captured by the youthful Captain John Trelawny, who found the presence of Gabriela a very pleasant surprise. He'd intended to return her on payment of hostage money but, before it could be paid, the handsome privateer had fallen in love with the exotic beauty and she with him. He carried her back with him to his Cornish castle and they were married.

When Cate was born, her father had called her his little Spanish princess and had renamed his ship in her honour. Growing up at Pentreath, Cate had been happy, with both parents watching over her progress with pleasure and anticipation.

Then her life had changed. Five years ago, when Cate reached the age of three and ten, her mother died. Disaster struck again when her father was killed.

Cate would not forget the slow death of her mother with a fever, but the day her father died was etched deeply on her brain. The pale sun shining through the windows of the castle's long gallery, the sloop anchored in haste on a flat grey sea, the crew splashing onto the shingles, their urgent shouts. Her father being carried in, weak and bloodied. His last word: Lovett.

She was startled out of her thoughts by the strains of a boisterous work chant.

The pirate ship — whose was it? That unusual flag. Her own privateer colours had a background of yellow from the House of Habsburg for her Spanish ancestry, with the King's Jack in the centre showing the union of England and Scotland. Some pirates had also started to use their own individual flags. Black was becoming common, with a symbol such as a skull and crossed bones to frighten other ships into surrender, but most pirates still flew the 'pretty red'. Cate's opponent's flag had been red, but with a difference. She frowned as she tried to focus on the image in her mind. Red, with the bold, black initial in the centre. She bit her lip. Was the letter an S, or perhaps an L? The script was certainly flamboyant, like the man himself.

Her thoughts moved to the pirate captain. Her crew, like most sailors, were of no more than average height, stocky and bearded. This man had been very different — tall and clean-shaven. The breadth of his shoulders suggested strength, yet he'd stood with an athletic grace. A flush rose to Cate's cheeks. The nerve of the man to sweep his hat off to her like that! She laughed softly, remembering his smile. It was a singularly sweet one for such a man, forming slowly and curving delightfully. Would any woman he kissed find his lips soft and gentle? What was she thinking? The man was her enemy, had challenged her, injured her crew and damaged her ship. She could make no sense of her reaction to him.

There was a tap on the door.

'Yes?' Cate sat up on the divan, pushing stray tendrils of hair from her warm face, as Morgan entered. 'Is there a problem?'

'No, ma'am. I wondered if the men could have an extra ration of rum.'

'Of course. And tell them they did well today.'

He nodded, scratched his beard and hesitated.

'Is there something else?' she asked.

'Only that, well, some of the men think the narrow escape we had — '

'Narrow escape?' Cate rose to her feet, her brows drawn. 'He was clever, I admit, but let me remind you we were the undisputed victors.'

Morgan took a step back. 'I know that, ma'am, but you know what men can be like.'

'What are you trying to say, Morgan?'

'The men respected your late father, as you know, so they never said anything about having a woman on board when you sailed with us. But ... '

'Yes?' Her voice carried a warning.

Morgan persisted. 'Well, they wondered why you didn't loot the enemy ship. It was there for our taking.'

She had no answer. Had she lost her nerve? She knew it could lead to dissension among the men. But that was her decision and not the men's business. 'We already have plunder in the hold from the French vessel. Wine, exotic spices, beautiful glass from Venice. These will earn good prize money for us all.' Morgan shrugged. 'My letter of marque gives authority to plunder merchant ships of countries at war with Britain. Not to hunt down pirates. A good captain will think of her men's safety and not unduly jeopardise their lives.' He made no reply and she glared at him. 'Is there someone who thinks they can do a better job than I?'

'It's not that, Cap'n.'

'Then what is it?'

He gave a short laugh. 'They think you might not be up to it on your own. That maybe you should take a husband.'

'A husband?' She moved to the table in the centre of the cabin, took a seat and motioned for Morgan to sit opposite.

'What is your thought on this?' Her voice was dangerously low as she gave him a sweet smile.

'I suppose it might not be a bad idea.'

'It would be for me.'

He grinned. 'My missus has no complaints with her marital state.'

'That's not what I've heard.' She matched his grin and he looked embarrassed. 'And how would a husband improve the situation you've just described?' Cate pushed a tankard in his direction and indicated he should help himself from the bottle on the table.

He poured a measure. 'The men think — I'm not saying I agree, you understand — that you need a more experienced man, to help you do a proper job, so to speak.'

'Let me remind you of Lady Mary Killigrew. She worked the seas over a hundred years ago, was the daughter of a pirate and was a successful pirate herself.'

Morgan took a deep draught from the tankard and wiped his mouth with the back of his hand. He leaned back in the chair. 'Mary Killigrew's husband was a pirate, so he could guide her.'

'Enough!' Cate leapt up, her cheeks hot. Morgan jumped, scraping the legs of his chair against the floor.

'Her husband was an ex-pirate,' she said. 'Take care that you don't become an ex-privateer. I am my father's daughter. He was a good captain and I intend to be just as good in my own right. I think you've said enough, Morgan. If any of the crew has a grievance, we will hold a meeting in the usual way. If not, I bid you good night.'

As her chief mate left he said over his shoulder, 'If you were one of my daughters — '

She picked up his empty tankard from the table and threw it with perfect aim at his backside. Not very ladylike, but what did she care?

2

The evening sky was streaked with gold-edged clouds as the Spanish Princess tossed over the waves. Cate leaned against the rail and thought of the man she'd seen through her spyglass. Was he now on the deck of his ship, having the same thoughts? But he was a man and there must be a certain camaraderie between him and his crew. There were times when she longed for someone she could be with as an equal. Why did the image of the pirate captain fly back to her? She was Catherine Trelawny of Pentreath Castle — that insolent creature could hardly be her equal!

Yet there was something attractive about his slow, sweet smile, the easy grace with which he swept her a bow. She blushed to herself in the dark, shook her head and went below to her cabin and to her bed.

*　*　*

Two days later, the Spanish Princess dropped anchor off Azul. The island's inhabitants spoke Spanish, a legacy of having been under Spanish rule for two hundred years. Cate felt at home here. Her mother had spoken to her in Spanish from the time Cate was a little girl and her father had continued to do so. 'It helps to keep alive your mother's memory,' he'd said.

Cate stood impatiently on deck, savouring the briny smell but eager to see the harbour town again. Her father had friends in Carpio Puerto who had always made them welcome. She saw ships of every size from different nations riding at anchor in the harbour. Sailors sang and called to each other as they made ready for sea, and others left their boats to go ashore and enjoy breakfast. Cate's stomach grumbled, reminding her she had not yet eaten this morning. Her mouth watered, relishing the thought of the sweet, juicy oranges piled on the quay.

She had dressed in a clean white loose shirt tucked into a long brown skirt. At her waist was a wide leather belt with a sheath hanging from it, and into this she slid her knife. Cate did not fear for her safety, but it was wise to be armed in harbour towns where pirates congregated. She lifted her canvas bag containing a few belongings and threw it onto the wooden pier below. Looping the fabric of her skirt over one arm, she climbed down the ladder over the side of the sloop and at the bottom jumped lightly onto the pier.

Morgan and others of her crew were already ashore and were looking eagerly around. From the open-fronted taverns along the bustling main street came the music of guitars and flutes. In the street a monkey danced to the music of a concertina. Stalls were set out to sell bright necklaces and bracelets, sandals and secondhand clothing. The air was filled with the mingled scents of spices drying in the sun.

'Organise provisions and whatever repairs are needed, Mr Morgan,' she said, 'Then you are free to enjoy yourself. Ensure a couple of men stay on board. Meet me here at the same time tomorrow to let me know of progress.'

'Aye, ma'am.' Morgan touched his cap and sauntered off to speak to the rest of the crew. They stood on the quay, calling out cheerfully to the young women who strolled past eyeing the men provocatively.

Cate left the harbour and, swinging her bag, wandered along the dusty cobbled street past the taverns and lodging houses popular with sailors. She reached the corner of the waterfront where it merged into a labyrinth of narrow streets and alleys. Here a small inn boasted a gaily-painted sign of an anchor, proclaiming it to be the Ancle Posada, the Anchor Inn. Its door stood open to the street and the din of conversations came through the doorway.

She stepped into the low-ceilinged room and a cloud of tobacco smoke greeted her. An old sailor with rings in both ears looked up from his cards and gave an appreciative whistle. The other drinkers raised their tankards and joined in.

'Hola!' Cate laughed. She glanced round at the men. They would have come from many sea-faring countries, but all spoke at least a smattering of Spanish. 'Donde esta Abella?' she asked.

The good-natured cry of 'Abella!' went up. Almost immediately a plump, weather-beaten woman of middle years came bustling out of a side room, wiping her hands on her apron.

'Sí, si. Qué es?' Her eyes fell on Cate. 'Catherina! Oh, I am so happy to see you!' She hastened over and embraced Cate. 'Come, please.' Abella took Cate by the hand and led her past the customers and through a door at the back of the inn, into her own small, comfortable parlour. 'Sit, sit. And you are well?'

Cate smiled and dropped her bag. 'I am. It's good to see you again.' She kissed the older woman's soft cheek. 'Can you keep a bed for me for tonight, Abella? I'd like to leave my bag here first and stretch my legs.'

'Sofia will ready a room,' Abella smiled. 'Join me for supper. We have much to talk bout.'

Cate thanked Abella and left the inn, turning inland. The buildings became further apart as the few streets rose in the hillside. Cobbles gave way to a sun-baked track and then to grasses. Goats were grazing on the sparse vegetation as the sun climbed higher in the sky. When she reached the top of the hill, Cate watched little crafts in the water below, sliding between the ships moored with their forest of masts.

Her curls lifted in the breeze. The sun beat down and Cate felt sleepy. She stretched out on the grass, put her hands behind her head and closed her eyes.

She woke when a shadow crossed her eyelids.

Cate's senses came flooding back. She gasped as she wrenched open her eyes. A tall figure stood over her, outlined in the rays of the sun. In an instant she sat up, feeling for the knife at her belt. Before she could pull the blade from its sheath, the man squatted beside her.

'Señorita,' he said, the English accent strong. 'I saw you lying here and was afraid you had taken ill. I see I was mistaken, for you look very well indeed.' There was amusement in his eyes.

Now he was close, she saw fair hair tied back from a strong, tanned face. His white shirt was open at the neck. Her eyes unconsciously travelled down to the fitted breeches, stretched taut across his thighs.

'I hope I am not intruding.' His voice was deep and warm.

'You are not, sir.' She met his look boldly, but kept her hand on her knife. 'This land belongs to no one, least of all me.'

'Indeed?'

'There is no one to tell us to leave his land, unlike in England. You are English, I think?'

'I am. And you, señorita, speak very good English, but I detect Spanish in your accent.'

'My father was English, my mother Spanish.'

'Ah.' He paused. 'May I sit for a while? My thighs are beginning to ache.' There was a twinkle in his eyes and Cate realised he was flirting with her. No doubt he thought her a woman of easy virtue, lying alone on the grass. She moved her hand from her knife, but her senses were alert as she answered him with a nod.

He lowered himself to the ground. 'What a delightful view.' He was not looking out to sea but at her and his eyes were laughing.

'Yes. It is where I come to do nothing,' she said, deliberately misunderstanding his implied meaning, 'And then, before I become too idle, I return to my usual life.'

'And what is that?' he asked casually.

'That, sir, is none of your business.' She had no intention of telling this man she was a privateer. Further, she was enough of a lady to recognise the situation she was in. 'I believe in England it is not considered proper for an unmarried woman to converse alone with a man when they have not been introduced.'

A muscle at the corner of his mouth twitched. 'My apologies. My name is Henry Darley. May I know your name?'

'I am Miss Catherina Trelawny.'

'I am pleased to meet you. There. We have dealt with the formalities, Miss Trelawny.' He flashed her a look she could not fathom, before turning his gaze seaward. 'There is nothing like this in England.'

'Sea surrounds most of England, Mr Darley.'

'That is true. I merely meant the sky is not so cloudless and the sea not so blue.'

Relaxing, she hugged her long brown skirt to her knees. 'Which part of England is your home?'

His smile showed even, white teeth in the tanned face. 'I am from Dorchester.'

'I was there once with my father.'

'Then you will be aware what a pleasant place it is.' He regarded her with curiosity.

She shook her head. 'I do not remember it well. It was long ago, when I was a young girl.'

'Then not so long ago.'

Cate laughed. 'You are ridiculous, sir.'

'And you are fortunate, Miss Trelawny, to live on such a beautiful island as this.'

Cate bit her lip. She would not correct his mistaken assumption. To tell him about her life was impossible. She regarded him. His face and frame were very pleasing. Perhaps Morgan was right about her taking a husband. She glanced down to hide a smile. As if such a man as this could be her companion on the high seas!

'What brings you to Azul, Mr Darley?' She raised her eyes again to meet his face. 'It is a long way from Dorchester.'

'It is. But I have a love of the sea and ships, and I am interested in many things in other countries. There are varieties of plants growing wild here I have heard of but never seen. I believe the bird of paradise is something to behold.'

'I can show you where one grows.' She spoke without thinking, proud of her knowledge of the island. He looked at her with such pleasure that her cheeks grew hot. 'If you'd like me to, that is.'

'I would be forever in your debt,' he said.

He was laughing at her, she was sure, but before she could decide how to respond he rose to his feet. The man was much taller than she had imagined. He held out his hand. Cate placed her hand in his warm, strong one, and he drew her up. 'You would like to see it now, sir?'

'If you have the time.'

She found she had no wish to refuse him. 'It is not far.'

They walked in silence, side by side, Cate suddenly shy and grateful for the roughness of the path which called for concentration. She glanced at him from under her lashes, trying to place him. He was English, and his accent and manners suggested a gentleman, but his plain clothes did not imply wealth. Yet his air was one of unconscious assurance,

36

as though he was accustomed to doing what he pleased in any company. They continued walking and she realised what made him different from other gentlemen. He wore his own hair, instead of the curled wigs that were the fashion. It suited him.

She stopped and pointed. 'There.'

The bird of paradise stood over six feet, as tall as he. On top of its long stem, spiky petals of brilliant orange resembled the comb of a cockerel, with a pink beak-like leaf below.

'It is even more exotic than I have heard tell,' he said, his voice soft.

'It's most beautiful in winter and early spring,' she said, 'But it flowers a number of times a year. When the sunbirds come to drink the nectar, the petals open to cover their feet in pollen.'

As he gazed at the plant, she stole another glance at him, studying his profile, the straight nose, the soft hair tucked behind his ear. He turned to her suddenly and she met his sea-blue eyes. Her heart gave a strange lurch.

'Thank you for showing me,' he said.

Embarrassed, she looked away. With a start, she noticed the sun was low in the sky. Below them the streets would be emptying of children and in the houses families would be gathering to eat their suppers.

'I must go. My friend is expecting me.'

She stood there, reluctant to move.

'Shall we meet again?' he asked.

'No doubt. Azul is a small island.'

He bowed, took her hand and kissed it. She found herself laughing at his deliberate formality.

Cate set off down the hill, the warm summer darkness falling. She glanced back. He stood there, watching her, looking remote, mysterious.

★ ★ ★

When Cate returned to the Ancle Posada Abella was busy with evening customers, so she called to her friend and made her way up the wooden staircase. The room was simply furnished, but neat red curtains hung at the windows and the floor was freshly swept. The inn's young maid brought up warm water.

'The missus sends these for you,' said the girl, spreading clean garments over the back of the chair before bobbing a curtsy and leaving.

Cate undressed, sank into the soapy water with a sigh of pleasure and closed her eyes. Unbidden, the handsome Mr Henry Darley entered her mind. Surely they would meet again?

She rose dripping from the bath, dried herself and slipped on a fresh chemise of her own. She lifted the other garments from the chair. A simply-cut bodice and full skirts of lemon silk.

Cate entered the kitchen as Abella, stirring a pot on the stove, looked up. 'You look very well.'

'Thank you for lending me this beautiful gown,' said Cate, smoothing the folds of the skirts.

'It is a gift,' Abella said. 'It will never fit me again. Ah, Cate — you will make some man a handsome wife one day.'

'Not you, too, Abella!' Cate laughed. 'I've already had marital advice from Mr Morgan.'

Abella lifted wooden plates from a cupboard and set them on the table. 'What did he say?'

'That I need a husband to guide me.'

'And what caused such impertinence?'

Cate pulled out a chair. 'The Spanish Princess was attacked a few days ago and, although we had the victory, I decided not to plunder the ship.'

Abella glanced at Cate. 'Hmm, well, that was your decision to make.'

'Yes, it was.'

'Bah! Men! They think they are so perfect.' Abella spooned spicy chicken onto the plates with such force that some of it splashed onto her scrubbed wooden table.

'Don't let the behaviour of men spoil our meal!' Cate laughed.

'You must be famished, child,' said Abella as they settled down to the meal.

'I've had enough of biscuits and salted

beef.'

'I heard about your father's death, mi amiga, and I am so sorry,' said Abella, reaching out to squeeze Cate's hand. 'He was a good man and a friend to me.'

'Thank you, Abella. It is hard sometimes without him.'

'And now you are captain of the Spanish Princess. He would be pleased to know you decided to do this.'

'Not having a mother made us close.'

'Yes, your poor mother. But she made you half-Spanish, which is a good thing!'

Cate laughed. 'That is true.'

In the pause that followed, muted sounds of men talking and clattering tankards filtered through to the kitchen where Cate and Abella sat.

'How are things here? Has there been any trouble with corsairs? I hear they have captured thousands of ships and even more people.'

Abella frowned. 'The mainland is often attacked by Barbary pirates, but we are lucky as they've not troubled this island for some years. There is gossip, though, that a corsair captain has moved his activities from the Caribbean to the Mediterranean. An Englishman — Solomon Green. He worked with his father in a London shipyard before turning pirate. But for now, our fishermen don't fear going to sea.'

The candles had burned low when the conversation returned to the attack on the Spanish Princess.

'So whose ship was this, which dared to attack you?' Abella drained her wine glass.

'A pirate sloop. Its colours were unusual. Red, but with a black initial in the centre.'

'What was the initial?'

Cate reached for the wine. 'An S, perhaps.'

'Are you sure? Could it have been an L?'

'It was an elaborately curled initial, so it might be as you say.' She frowned at her friend. 'Why do you ask?'

Abella shrugged. 'The only flag I have

heard of that description has the letter L for the pirate captain, Lovett.'

'Lovett ... ' Cate felt the colour drain from her face. 'Oh, how could I have been so stupid?' She put down the wine bottle and was suddenly stone-cold sober.

'What is it, Cate?' said Abella, alarmed, as Cate reached out and clutched her hand.

'What does this man, Lovett, look like?' she said quickly. 'Describe him to me.'

'I don't know him myself. Many people come and go on this island and it is often best not to ask questions. But you hear all sorts of things in an inn. He's been described as tall and wearing all black, save for a red feather in his hat.'

Cate slumped back into the chair. 'It is the same man. The one I fought just a few days ago. The man who killed my father.'

'Cate, how do you know this?'

She struggled to keep her voice under control. 'My father would not take me on what was to be his last voyage, although I begged him to. He said it was dangerous — more dangerous than usual. Then came the day with shouting and running footsteps, and the dreadful moment when my father was carried into the great hall, barely conscious.'

She paused to steady her breathing and continued. 'The men lowered him onto the settle by the fireplace. The front of his shirt was discoloured by blood and infection.' Her voice faltered again. 'I ran to him and knelt at his side, and his eyelids flickered open. His breath was harsh and his face the colour of parchment. When he spoke my name, his voice came cracked and painful. I begged him not to talk, took his limp hand — and, oh, his skin was so cold.' Cate's heart beat faster as she re-lived the moment. 'He was struggling to keep his eyes focused. His voice was little more than a whisper, but I heard him clearly. He said, 'Lovett.' I raised his hand and pressed it to my cheek. His eyes closed and he was no more ... '

'Cate, are you sure — ?'

'Yes, Morgan told me the whole story!'

'Then this pirate captain is dead?'

asked Abella, her voice tense. Cate buried her face in her hands. 'No, he is not. I wish he were!'

'My dear, do not distress yourself any more.'

Cate lifted a drained face. 'I fear that only revenge will soothe my feelings, Abella.'

'Hush, child, you are not yourself to be saying such nonsense.'

'He waved to me as we sailed away. The next time we meet, I will tell him I am the daughter of John Trelawny and that I intend to see my father's murderer swing on the gallows!'

3

Henry woke to sun filtering through the shutters, dust motes dancing in the light. Already the air was thickening with the day's heat. Languidly he stretched his long limbs. The sheet slipped to his waist, exposing broad shoulders and a tracing of fair hair on his chest. Henry turned onto his side, leaned head on elbow, and surveyed the room.

It contained only the basic furnishings, but it was cleaner than he was used to at such inns and the woman who ran it was a pleasant soul. The rest of his crew had chosen to stay at the harbour end of town, where there were a number of women who were set on pleasing them.

Henry had only one woman on his mind: Miss Catherina Trelawny.

At first he had not recognised the Spanish Princess, for if he had he would have stayed the order to attack. Once she had raised the distinctive British-Spanish flag, he knew — and was astonished, for John Trelawny was dead.

Trelawny had been killed during an attack on the Spanish Princess off the coast of France some six months earlier. Henry had heard the report at a tavern when he passed through Cornwall and had been saddened.

Who, then, was sailing his ship?

Had the Spanish Princess been sold or was it still in the hands of the Trelawny family? With a start, he'd remembered Trelawny's daughter.

As the noise of the battle had raged around him, he'd hesitated, torn between regard for the memory of Trelawny and awareness of his own role as pirate captain. Could Catherina Trelawny really be on that ship, giving the orders?

Another cannon boom had brought Henry up sharply. Whoever it was, they were fighting back. So Henry gave the order to fight on, but he took care to minimise the damage to the other sloop and the danger to those on board. Then

47

he had seen a woman on deck. He'd pulled out his spyglass and watched her, as she'd watched him through a spyglass of her own.

Remembering that now, Henry smiled. He saw again her laughing response to his salutation at her victory. He rolled onto his back, slid his hands behind his head and his smile broadened.

Young Catherina had turned into a beauty! He had not seen her since John Trelawny visited Henry's family home, bringing his little daughter with him. Henry tried to remember how old he must have been then. A young man of four and ten years, just before he ran away to sea. She had seemed to him then a strange child, some eight years younger than he, with her wild black hair and unfamiliar accent. Catherina must now be eight and ten, and was clearly a resourceful young lady.

Henry sighed, regretting his action in attacking her ship. When the Oceanus had moored in Azul harbour, he'd seen the Spanish Princess. Immediately he'd decided to seek out Catherina and make himself known to her and offer his condolences on the death of Trelawny.

He'd given his men shore leave, deposited his small bag of belongings in the Ancle Posada and set off through the town. The town of Carpio Puerto was not large and it shouldn't take long to find her. Then he had seen a young woman striding up the hill, her hips swinging, one hand lifting the glossy black curls from her neck.

He followed her, but why had he not revealed his identity when they first spoke? It had seemed amusing to him, to see if she recognised him. Of course she had not; how could she after all these years when she had been so young at the time? He had let pass the opportunity and now she thought of him as a stranger. Henry flushed at the memory of Catherina's sun-warmed skin. Her accent was enchanting, and ah, those velvety dark eyes! A smile touched his lips.

He brought his mind back to the present. Today he would find Miss Trelawny again and reveal his true identity.

The smell of frying bacon wafted up the stairs. Henry threw off the sheet, padded across the floorboards and poured water from the jug into the washing bowl. He washed, dressed and ran down to the parlour, where loud conversation and the clattering of dishes greeted him.

He ate hungrily. Fresh air, exercise and weeks on a ship's diet had given him an appetite.

No sooner had he finished breakfast than Catherina entered the parlour. She glanced around, saw him and walked towards him, her sparkling eyes meeting his. Henry rose from his seat. As she approached, watching him with a smile, he thought her face was the most expressive and beautiful one he had ever seen.

'Miss Trelawny.' The desire to press his lips against the warm skin of her throat was so strong that he almost shuddered. She was looking at him with a quizzical expression. He cleared his throat and smiled. 'How pleasant to see you again this morning, Miss Trelawny.'

'Good morning to you, Mr Darley.'

Ah, thought Henry, *this is my cue. But not like this, standing here.*

'Will you join me in a cup of coffee?' He indicated his table beside the window.

'You are taking breakfast here?'

'It is my lodging for the time being.'

'I would like coffee,' she said, meeting his eyes. 'Thank you.'

He pulled out a chair for her and took a seat opposite.

Abella, her hair tidied into a purple silk turban, moving about the room with a cheerful word for each guest, reached Cate and Henry. She glanced from one to the other. 'Catherina, Señor Darley ... you know each other?'

'A little,' said Cate.

'Quite well,' said Henry at the same time.

Abella burst into laughter. 'While you make up your mind, what can I get you?'

'Two coffees, por favor, Abella,' said Henry.

As they waited, Cate's lashes lowered

while she appeared to be studying the table, and he studied her. He still liked what he saw. The morning sun caught her raven hair, and one of her smooth curls had slipped forward and lay against her breast. Henry wanted to see her eyes again, and she obliged him by looking up suddenly. Yes, they were very dark, like liquid. She flushed and Henry's composure slipped. What must she think of him, staring at her? He was saved from comment by Abella's return, placing the coffee jug and two mugs on their table.

'Are you going to the gathering at Nicolas Lopez's tonight?' Abella asked Cate.

'Gathering?' said Henry.

'Like a troil in Cornwall is held to celebrate a good fishing season,' said Cate. 'Music and singing, dancing and story-telling.'

'Mr Darley? Will you join us?' Abella asked.

Henry grinned. 'How could I resist an evening in such pleasant company as the two of you?'

With a satisfied smile, Abella left them alone again. Few customers now remained in the parlour, and those were seated on the other side of the room. Muted street noises of passing barrows, the clipping of horse hooves and snatches of conversations floated in through the open door.

'Abella knows you well,' said Henry, as Cate poured the aromatic coffee.

'I am fortunate to have her as a friend.'

'And I am fortunate to have met you again.'

'You make pretty little speeches,' she said.

'It suits the company in which I find myself.' He raised his mug to her.

'What really brings you to Azul. sir?'

'A natural curiosity, Miss Trelawny.'

'And is it satisfied?'

'Oh, not yet, madam!'

What was it about this young woman that made him feel inordinately pleased as she laughed and glanced at him over the rim of her coffee?

'There is much to enjoy on the island,'

she said. 'How long will you be staying?'

'That depends,' he said, a smile in his voice.

'On what?'

'I'm not sure yet.' He watched her closely. 'Do you live on the island?'

'No, just a visitor from time to time.'

'And where do you live when not here?'

'You are curious again, Mr Darley.' Her eyes met his. 'You are the strangest man,' she said. 'Why do you question me?'

'Because I like to hear your voice,' he said with perfect honesty.

'I am deeply flattered.'

He saw an unmistakable twinkle in her dark eyes and knew with a jolt of pleasure that she was teasing him. He broke into laughter and she joined him.

'I must apologise for my impertinent comment,' she said at last. She looked grave. 'May I speak to you on a serious matter?'

'Of course,' said Henry. The uncomfortable notion flashed through his mind that she had discovered he was her recent adversary.

But it seemed not, for when she spoke again, she said, 'I have a favour to ask of you.'

Henry inclined his head. 'Your servant, señorita.'

'It is a delicate matter.' She paused and began again. 'Sir, you are an Englishman and a man of the sea.' Bemused, he nodded. 'It's a long story and I do not wish to burden you with it,' she continued, embarrassment in her voice, 'But I would be grateful if could you help me find an English pirate by the name of Lovett.'

'Lovett?' Henry fought to maintain a polite expression on his face and to make sense of what she had said. Catherina wanted to find him? He should say, *I am that man.* But there was loathing in her eyes. Surely he had done nothing to deserve such hatred?

'Yes,' she said. 'Have you heard of him?'

He managed a short laugh. 'Indeed, I have.'

'It is no laughing matter!' Her eyes flashed.

Was this some kind of a joke? 'I think most sea-going men have heard of him.' Henry clicked his tongue in mock disapproval. 'He is something of a rogue, I understand.'

'A rogue?' She rose abruptly, her fists clenched by her side. 'That is too generous. He is a monster!'

Henry jumped to his feet. 'Miss Trelawny, my most sincere apologies. I did not mean to make light of whatever this man has done to you.'

He didn't have to pretend dismay. His heart thudded. He couldn't deny the feelings for her that were stirring in his breast, but she wanted nothing to do with him. That is, with the pirate Lovett. What had his other self done? She clearly didn't associate him with the attack on her ship.

She resumed her seat.

He said, puzzled, 'What is the reason for your dislike of him?'

'More than dislike. I hate him.'

Henry could not keep his astonishment out of his voice. 'Hate is a strong word.'

Tears sprang to her eyes and she brushed them away with her hand, until at last she was able to speak.

'All you need to know is that I must find him. I believe he is on the island. Will you help me?' He wanted to see her again and he needed to learn more before revealing his identity. 'Yes.' He nodded. 'If I hear talk of Lovett's whereabouts, I will let you know.' Cate rose and turned towards the door. Henry stood and watched her walk out into the street. What in heaven's name was he supposed to have done?

★ ★ ★

Cate turned the corner of the street into the cool shade of a narrow alley. Deep in thought, she stumbled on a cobble and did not see the man until it was too late. He reached out and caught her by the elbow.

'Take care, madam.'

Cate saw a tall, thin man of perhaps fifty years, beads of perspiration on his forehead, wearing the neckerchief, loose jacket and baggy breeches of a sailor. 'You are not ill, I trust?' he asked.

'No, I thank you for your concern.'

He bowed. 'Jake Elphick.' A scar from his mouth to his chin produced a lopsided grin.

Cate felt a small pain under her ribs. Her father had a similar smile, the result of a badly-done tooth extraction. She felt a warmth towards the stranger. His name was vaguely familiar, too. Perhaps something had father had told her?

'Your name seems known to me, sir.'

'I am certain we have never met before.' He smoothed his thinning sandy-coloured hair. 'May I know your name?'

'Miss Trelawny.'

The man's flushed face darkened and he said suddenly, 'If there is no further assistance I can give, I bid you good-day.'

Dismissing him from her thoughts, she strode through the narrow streets, exchanging polite greetings with women seated outside their open doors, mending nets. Cate walked with swinging strides along the line of the coast, until she reached a rough, narrow path leading to a small, shingle beach. She scrambled down. The sun beat on her bare head and it was a relief to see a cool, damp cave. At its mouth lay a shallow, sunlit pool. Slipping off her soft leather sandals, she stepped into the warm water. There came only the hush of the far waves and she felt tension ebbing away through her feet on the sandy floor.

Soon the cave drew her and she wandered into its cool interior. A narrow shaft of light spilled from above and she saw at the rear a narrow staircase. Intrigued, Cate strapped on her sandals and stepped across the damp floor.

The stair twisted around to the right. As her eyes adjusted, she could make out each uneven step had been hewn from the rock. She stepped onto the first tread. The sea roared in, crashed over her and lifted her up. She choked as it dashed her against the rocky back wall. Her head throbbing, she fought to breathe as the sea washed over her.

Cate came up to the surface, gulping in air and thrashing her arms. She clung to the side of the rock, water swirling about her breast. The roof was barely two feet above her head. Bright sunlight at the cave mouth was tantalisingly visible, but the sea inside was swelling and heaving, and she couldn't move towards the entrance.

Desperately drawing in air, she looked frantically around for the stairs she'd seen. Over there — not too far. She struggled against the weight of her sodden skirts and dragged herself up half a dozen steps and out of the water. Shivering, she slumped down.

When her breathing grew less ragged, Cate crawled higher up the slimy, pitted steps. Her heartbeat less painful, she followed the rough staircase. It turned, the steps getting smaller but the air growing fresher and warmer. At last came a faint lifting of the darkness and she breathed more deeply. At the top of the tunnel, natural light filtered through a wide crack. As she reached it, a face appeared. Cate drew back. It was a vision from hell with its glistening eyes and twisted mouth. It spoke. 'Miss Trelawny.'

She recognised the features of the man she had met a short while ago. He reached his hand into the hole and drew her out onto the sunny cliff-face.

Wincing, she took her hands from his grasp and saw red grazes which throbbed. Water dripped from her clothes.

'You are wet,' he said, 'And hurt.'

'It's nothing.'

'How fortunate that I was taking a stroll on the cliff. I noticed this crevice, heard noises — and there you were.'

'I was also out for a walk, when a fierce wave washed me into a cave and I couldn't get out. I saw light, followed the stairs and you appeared.'

'The steps were undoubtedly made by smugglers.' He pressed his lips together and took a step towards her.

'Hola!'

He whirled round at the shout.

Abella's brother waved cheerfully from a distance, as he came puffing towards them. 'I thought it was you, Cate. I've some tasty young seabirds from the nests in the cliff-face for my supper.' He indicated his hessian sack.

'Alberto,' said Cate, a little relieved. She hadn't liked the way Mr Elphick stepped forward.

'Your clothes are wet through,' said Alberto. 'Did you fall into the sea?'

'Something like that,' said Cate with a smile.

'Let's walk back to town together.' Alberto offered his arm and she linked hers into it.

'Goodbye, Mr Elphick,' she said.

'Perhaps I could join you,' he said. 'I'm going that way.'

She had no choice but to nod in reply and stepped onwards with Alberto. Elphick placed himself on the other side of Cate. Alberto whistled softly as they walked.

Cate didn't want to encourage the

man in any way, but she wanted to learn whatever she could about Lovett. Eventually she said, 'I see from your clothes that you are a sailor, sir.'

'I am.'

She lowered her voice. 'There is an English sailor who I believe is at present on the island and I wonder if you know of him?'

'What is his name?'

'Lovett.'

Mr Elphick faltered in his stride. 'May I ask why you want to find Lovett?' He smiled and again that crooked smile tugged at her heart.

'It is a private matter, but he has done my father a great wrong.'

Elphick came to a halt, and Cate and Alberto were brought to a standstill. 'I do know the name. I've heard talk of Lovett on the ship where I am chief mate.'

'What do they say of him?' she said in a low voice to Elphick.

He grimaced. 'That he is from a respectable family but is a man gone bad.'

She caught her breath. Yes, she could believe that. Heat flooded her body. 'Do you know where I can find him?'

'I should be able to tell you shortly.'

Silence fell between them. A gull shrieked overhead, dragging her thoughts from anger onto more pleasant matters. Tonight was the gathering. Mr Darley said he would come. Perhaps they would dance together. Her heart beat faster.

The sounds of Carpio Puerto reached them. 'I will leave you here,' she said to Elphick, stopping where the narrow streets of the town began.

A small voice sounded in Cate's head. In trusting this stranger she might be letting her desire for revenge overcome her common sense. Well, as soon as she'd found Lovett and taken action, that would be the end of the matter.

'You can reach me at the Ancle Posada,' she said, and turned Alberto in that direction.

'I didn't like him,' said Alberto.

Cate bid Alberto farewell at the door to the inn and walked down to the quay.

She found Morgan supervising repairs to the Spanish Princess.

'When is work likely to be finished?' she said.

'One or two more days,' he told her.

'Does the delay in sailing have anything to do with the men wanting to prolong their shore leave?' she asked, suppressing a smile.

Morgan shook his head. 'All necessary repair work, ma'am.' He grinned.

Cate did not mind. It would allow more time to find Lovett. And more time to see Mr Darley.

★　★　★

It was well past mid-day when she returned to the Ancle Posada. She finished her meal and pushed away the empty plate. Leaning back in the chair, she was planning her own search for Lovett that afternoon when Abella appeared.

'A gentleman to see you, Catherina.' Abella raised her eyebrows, as if the visitor wasn't quite the gentleman he believed himself to be.

'Which one?' She sat up straight.

'How many gentlemen visitors are you expecting?' Cate laughed and rose from the table. 'He gave the name Elphick,' said Abella.

'I'll see him.'

'My dear,' Abella's usually cheerful face was creased in worry, 'I hope you are not getting into any sort of trouble?'

'More trouble than being a privateer?' Cate quirked an eyebrow at her friend.

'I mean it, mi amiga. Your father, God rest his soul,' Abella crossed herself, 'would never forgive me if anything happened to you.'

'I know what I am doing, Abella. I am trying to find out what I can about Lovett.'

'No good can come of this. Revenge causes only unhappiness.' She frowned. 'It may even end in death.'

'Lovett's death, I hope.' Cate spoke in a light tone but her heart was hard.

'Will you kill him?' Abella folded her arms across her chest. 'With your own bare hands?'

Cate shrugged. 'I might let the British authorities deal with him.'

'So you intend to capture him and take him back to England? How do you propose to do that?'

'I just want justice, Abella.'

'I know, my dear. But how are you going to prove his guilt? If he is indeed guilty?'

'Of course he is! And, oh — I don't know! One thing at a time, my friend.'

Abella took Cate's hands and kissed her cheek. 'I've asked Sofia to put Elphick in the back parlour. Leave the door ajar and you can call if you need me.'

'You're a good friend, Abella.' Cate was touched by Abella's concern, but she had to deal with this herself. She made her way to the little room at the rear of the inn, reserved for customers who paid extra for privacy, and pushed open the door.

Elphick's back was half-turned towards Cate. He stood in front of the inn's maid, his fingers toying with the small crucifix at her breast. Cate saw the girl's downcast eyes and trembling lip.

Cate stepped in and spoke curtly. 'Mr Elphick.'

His hand flew to his side as he spun round. Sofia threw a grateful look at Cate and ran from the room.

She despised men who preyed on those more vulnerable. Elphick was clearly nothing like her father. Why had she not noticed before the man's cold eyes?

Cate remained standing, so he was forced to do the same. 'Do you have some information for me, sir?' she asked in a cool voice.

'You indicated there might be some sort of reward ... You said you would be most obliged.' He gave a wide grin, disclosing yellowed teeth.

She raised her eyebrows. 'And what were you expecting in return for the information?'

'Nothing of any consequence, madam, I assure you! Only, perhaps, allow me to kiss your hand.'

A wave of disgust flooded over Cate.

A kiss on the back of a lady's hand was something that a gentleman might be allowed to do. And now she knew this man was not a gentleman.

He stepped forward. 'Lovett was seen off the coast of Sicily two days ago. His ship was attacked by another and some damage done.'

Cate nodded. She knew this much already.

'There is something else,' he said. 'It's rumoured that he attacks English ships, even though he's English himself. Worse, he's known for ambushing ships lying at anchor and dispatching the crew without a thought.'

The blood drained from her face and she sank down onto the small sofa. He was referring to her father's murder.

Elphick lowered himself next to her. 'Miss Trelawny, I am sorry to bring you this news,' he said softy. 'I saw the Spanish Princess in the harbour. Was John Trelawny a relative of yours?'

'He was my father.' She looked at Elphick's face and saw no surprise there.

'What do you know of the circumstances of my father's death?'

'Only the story that he was killed in an ambush off the French coast. And the man who killed him was working on the French ship. Henry Lovett.'

Elphick had confirmed Morgan's account and her father the name.

'Is Lovett on that ship?' Her mouth was dry.

'No, he now owns his own vessel.'

She nodded, cold stealing across her heart. 'And where is his ship now?'

'Here, moored for repairs.'

Of course. It was damaged in the battle and would need repairs. She had not been thinking clearly enough recently. Cate steadied herself and rose from the sofa.

'Thank you, Mr Elphick.'

He stood. 'Delighted to be of service. I will, of course, inform you if I learn anything further.'

Preoccupied with her thoughts, she barely noticed Elphick raise one of her hands to his lips.

4

Cate intended to go to the harbour and look for Lovett's sloop, but her head ached badly. She climbed the stairs, stripped off her brown skirts and spread them over the wooden chair. She lay down on her bed and closed her eyes, meaning only to rest for while. Almost immediately darkness rushed up.

Cate woke slowly, aware of the chattering and clattering below. The light in her room had changed. It must be early evening.

There came a soft knock at her door. 'Señorita. It's Sofia. The mistress asked me to bring you up hot water and to ask if you wanted any help getting ready for this evening.'

The gathering! Cate scrambled out of bed. She opened the door just wide enough to take a jug from the girl. 'Thank you, Sofia.'

Thank goodness her headache had

gone. She intended to enjoy every minute of this evening.

Cate hung her head over the bowl and tipped hot water over her hair, washing away the dirt and dust of the day, and sponged her body, removing the dried salt water that clung to her skin.

She lifted the lemon silk skirts Abella had given her and stepped into them. She swirled the fabric round her lower limbs, as if she were already dancing with Henry Darley, and her stomach fluttered. With a soft laugh, she turned to the bodice. Raising her arms, she slipped the short-sleeved garment over her head. Tugging it onto position, she laced up the front and tied a bow with trembling fingers. Each silky item was deliciously cool against her warm skin.

She peered into the small looking glass propped up on the dresser and saw a young woman with flushed cheeks, her eyes shining in anticipation at the evening to come. *I'm behaving like a smitten girl*, she thought.

Cate hastened to Nicolas Lopez's tavern. Groups of people were making their way in the same direction, jesting with one another. At the corner of a narrow lane stood a low timber-framed house, the door open to the warm evening air. Music, singing and laughter spilled out.

She slipped inside. Someone was playing a cheerful tune on an accordion, while the smiling Nicolas, jerkin stretched tight over his belly, sang in a raucous voice. He broke off to call, 'Welcome!' before throwing himself back into the song.

Long, rough-hewn tables and benches were set around the edges of the room, many of them already occupied. Across flickering candles pressed onto tin plates, Cate saw Abella and her brother seated at one of the tables. There was no sign of Mr Darley. Her stomach twisted a little. Affecting nonchalance, Cate strolled over to them and dropped into a chair.

'Nicolas is an enthusiastic singer, bless him,' she said, raising her voice above the din. Abella laughed, and Alberto called over a red-faced boy scuttling between kitchen and tables. In one hand the youth ferried a large jug of beer and in the fingers of his other hand he grasped the handles of empty pewter mugs.

Alberto gestured to Cate. 'Drink for my friend,' he said to the boy, 'and top us up while you're here.' The boy set down another mug and hastily poured three beers, before scuttling off to serve other tables.

'Has Mr Darley arrived?' asked Cate, her eyes searching. Some of her crew were carousing on the other side of the room. She was dismayed to see Elphick lounging alone against the back wall, a drink in his hand, staring across the room at her. Resolutely, she turned from him.

'He's not here yet,' said Abella.

'Who?' asked Alberto, wiping beer froth from his moustache.

'Cate has a gentleman friend,' said Abella with a smile.

'No,' protested Cate. The heat rose in her body. 'That is — '

'There he is,' said Abella.

Cate's heart lurched and seemed to swell within her breast. Henry Darley ducked his head under the low lintel and straightened. Her pulse quickened. Would he see her and come to the table? She held her breath, her cheeks colouring.

He glanced round the room, caught sight of her and weaved between the busy tables. She softly let out her breath.

'It's lively here,' he said, sliding into a seat beside Cate.

'It will get even livelier before the evening is out,' she said, feeling bold again.

The serving boy reappeared, poured another tankard of beer for Henry and moved on. Abella introduced her brother and Henry to each other. Nicolas finished his song and was greeted by loud cheering and banging on the tables. The accordion player struck up another tune.

'It's a reel,' said Henry, getting to his feet. He held out his hand to Cate. 'Let's dance.'

Men and women were already forming circles of eight and Henry tugged Cate into one of the groups. She saw Morgan drag Abella into another circle, while Alberto sank happily into his drink. Those not dancing were foot-stamping and clapping in time to the beat.

Then they were off, linking hands and flying round in one direction, then spinning in the other. Weaving in and out around the circle, they came together smiling, separated and met again. Cate was pushed into the centre of the circle to dance alone, her cheeks growing hot with pleasure and her curls flying wildly about her head. She zigzagged in and out of the circle, round each man in turn, and back into the centre each time, laughing and breathless. She rejoined the circle and Henry was thrust into the centre. He threw his arms above his head, threading between each of the women, one after the other, until Cate pulled him back into the circle.

'Let the other men have a go,' she scolded with a laugh.

The music grew louder, the men danced round faster and faster, and Cate's feet flew under her. At last the reel finished and they came to a halt.

'Excellent,' grinned Henry, as Cate, breathless, leaned against his beating chest, her cheeks so flushed she thought she'd never cool down. His sparkling eyes held hers and she felt no shyness, only pleasure.

He led her back to the table. Alberto dozed in contentment. Abella was chatting to friends across the room. Elphick had gone.

'This is proving a delightful evening,' she said.

'Delightful,' Henry repeated, not taking his eyes off her.

She couldn't stop a smile twitching at her lips. Henry, watching her mouth, at once became serious and he drew in his breath as if he were about to say something. 'Come,' he said softly, and led her to a small corner table, where a single candle burned low. They sat opposite each other and she looked at him, the candlelight highlighting his strong features, his straight nose, the lock of hair falling over his brow. His smile was as soft as a caress. Her heart quickened in her chest.

'You are light on your feet for such a tall man,' she managed to say.

He inclined his head. 'Merci, mademoiselle.'

'Tu parle Francais?'

'Un peu.'

'You told me yesterday that you were a voyager,' she said. 'Tell me about your travels.'

'Are you not something of a traveller yourself?'

'Not really,' she said, keeping her voice light.

'Where would you like me to begin?'

'Wherever you wish.'

The room was noisy and they had to lean towards each other to be heard. The music and chatter seemed to fade as he told her about Venice and its canals, the paintings in the churches and the wonderful food, the Gothic architecture of the Doge's Palace and the lagoon. Henry leaned further forward. 'The Piazza San Marco is a most splendid sight,' he said. His lips brushed against her ear, sending sparks through her body. 'Are you sure you're not bored?' he asked.

'Oh, no!' She could listen to him forever.

He talked about the Leeward Islands, its songs, plants and creatures. 'The strangest lizards you have ever seen — green, the length of a man, with a third eye on top of their heads.' As he spoke, his whole face lit up. She sat there with her chin on her hand, feasting on the stories and images.

There came a loud burst of laughter as a man slid off his chair and disappeared under the table. She was again aware of the room around them. She wanted to go back, to stay in that time forever, but it was too late.

'I love your stories,' she said. For all her sailing in the Spanish Princess over these last five years, she had visited few countries, travelling only on the routes known to her father.

'I can tell you more another day,' he said.

She bit her lip. 'We won't meet again once you have left the island.'

'You can't know that,' he said with a smile.

A small sigh escaped her. 'We'll both be back at sea soon.'

A shadow crossed his face in acknowledgement of this. 'Thank you for this evening with you.'

A smile touched her lips. 'I can't remember when I've enjoyed an evening more.'

Henry reached his hand across the small table and took hers in it. His eyes were warm. 'The pleasure was all mine, Miss Trelawny.'

Cate felt trapped in the blue depths of his gaze. Their lips were so close. She drew in a breath and leaned closer. Turning her face up to his, she waited shamelessly for what she hoped he would do next.

'Cate,' broke in Abella. She stood at

their table, smiling and mopping her brow.

Cate started, pulling her hand out of Henry's grasp. He got to his feet, politely, and she was left with a sudden sense of emptiness.

'What an evening it's been!' said Abella. 'I'm going back to the inn now,' she continued, oblivious to the emotion between Cate and Henry.

Cate saw now that people were leaving, throwing handfuls of coins onto tables as they did.

'I'll be along shortly,' she said, unwilling for the evening to end.

When Abella had gone, they called their thanks to Nicolas as he and the serving boy gathered up the tankards, and they went out into the night. They walked in companionable silence the short distance to the Ancle Posada. A few remaining revellers staggered homewards, while the waves washed against the sea-wall with a low sigh.

They entered the inn and at the bottom of the stairs, Henry turned to Cate.

'Goodnight, Catherina. I hope we will meet again.' He tenderly tucked a curl behind her ear.

'Goodnight,' she whispered, then turned and ran up the stairs to her room. A few minutes later, she heard his soft footsteps stop outside her door. She stood, waiting for him to knock, but he continued up the second flight of stairs.

Cate sank onto the bed. Her cheeks flamed at the thought of what she might, just now, so easily have done. She raised her chin, in some sort of defiance at herself, and caught a glimpse in the mirror of her sparkling eyes and dishevelled hair.

What had happened to her this evening? Her heart was suffused with happiness!

Cate could not sleep. Her room was stifling after the heat of the day and her thoughts were only of Henry Darley. She propped herself up in bed. He was everything a man should be — handsome and strong, kind and amiable. Their acquaintance may be short, but she was in danger of falling in love with him. She imagined being held in his arms, her hands sliding up his bare chest, travelling over his broad shoulders and around his neck, pulling his head down as his lips sought hers.

Cate took a deep breath to steady her racing pulse. Her time on Azul was coming to an end. And there was also the promise she had made, to herself and to her dead father.

She pulled back the sheet, crossed the room and threw open the shutters. Standing at the window, she half-listened to the song of cicadas as she tried to order her thoughts. She must put Henry out of her mind, at least until she had discovered if Lovett's ship was indeed moored in the harbour.

Decision made, Cate pulled on her shirt and loose dark trousers, and slipped out of her room, down the stairs and into the night. The pale light of a crescent moon bathed the streets and buildings. The blissful coolness of the air fanned her skin and went some way towards soothing her. Here and there a solitary man was out, carousing with a woman, but they were too preoccupied with each other to show any interest in Cate as she passed.

She reached the sea-wall. Palm trees threw long black shadows across the cobbles and she heard the low sigh of the sea, saw its dark surface glistening in the thin moonlight. If Elphick's information was correct, somewhere along the quay should be Lovett's sloop. She hoped Mr Darley hadn't forgotten his promise to help.

Suddenly she became aware of heavy breathing behind her. She spun round, pulling the knife from her belt. Staring at her with narrowed eyes was a man with a scar from eye to ear, a knife glittering in his hand. Cate's breath caught in her throat. The stranger stepped forward, not taking his eyes from her face. She crouched, putting all her weight onto the balls of her feet and held her knife towards him.

'Prepare to meet your maker,' he hissed.

'Not yet,' she said, keeping her voice steady as she watched for his next move.

His blade flashed towards her throat. She jumped to the side and the tip slit her sleeve.

She screamed as she slipped sideways and fell. Her knife skittered across the cobblestones just beyond her reach.

Then he was on her. Cate felt a great surge of energy as he thrust his blade towards her neck. She kicked his hand, knocking him off balance, grabbed it with both hands, brought it to her mouth and bit down hard. He dropped the knife, cursing, and she scrambled away. He grabbed the leg of her pantaloons, dragged her back and straddled her, his hands on her throat, his thumbs pressing on her wind-pipe, choking her. She searched for something on the ground to act as a weapon and her fingers closed upon a large stone. Gripping it tight, she drove it into his head. He yelled out, his hands shooting to where the blood flowed, and fell sideways onto the ground. She dropped the stone, heaved him from her and pushed herself back, kicking at him. As she stood, her knees trembling, he pulled himself along the ground, his glazed eyes upon her, a hand pressed to the wound in his head.

Her breath came ragged and she stepped further away as he struggled upright, the knife again in his hand. He came towards her and she backed away towards the edge of the sea-wall. His breath came short as he launched himself at her. She sidestepped, he staggered and fell, his arms circling wildly as he tried to keep his balance. Their eyes met for a moment as he toppled over the sea-wall. Cate stood motionless as he hit the water with a splash, her heart thumping.

'Miss Trelawny!'

She whipped round at the sound of the voice. Elphick stepped towards her, his features barely distinguishable in the weak light of the lantern he held raised.

'Mr Elphick,' she said, her voice hoarse.

'You are in some difficulty?'

She pointed to the water. 'He tried to kill me.'

Elphick moved to the edge of the sea-wall and held his lantern over the water. She followed him and peered into the dark sea, illuminated in the small pool of yellow light. The shape of the man was just visible, as he flailed and splashed towards the jetty. He dragged himself up the steps and stumbled away into the dark alleys at the other end of the harbour.

'Stop him,' she croaked. 'He is wounded and cannot go far.'

'I am sorry you had to experience that, Miss Trelawny,' said Elphick. 'Some men cannot hold their drink. As you are accustomed to ships and their men, you must know that.'

'It was more than a drunk man's wild behaviour!' She reached for Elphick's lantern. 'If you won't go after him, I will.'

He moved the lamp out of her reach. 'Come now, Miss Trelawny, I doubt it was quite like that. Allow me to escort you back to your lodging.'

Cate saw her knife at the edge of the circle of light and snatched it up. It was too late now to go after her assailant, Elphick had seen to that. Again, he had appeared at an opportune moment. Even if the first occasion, when she had tripped on a cobblestone, had been by chance — and she had to allow that was likely — the other two occasions were surely not. Although he could not have known a wave would sweep her into the cave, that he was there suggested he'd been following her. But why? He'd stepped towards her on the cliff top, then Alberto had come along and whatever Elphick had intended did not happen.

'Another fortuitous appearance, Mr Elphick.'

'My dear lady, I had hoped you would not comment on that. The fact is, I was haggling with a doxy. She ran off as soon as you screamed.'

Cate hadn't seen or heard anyone run off. How long had Elphick been in the shadows? A lantern can be covered to obscure its light.

'Thank you, sir, but I do believe I am safe, for the time being,' she said carefully.

'At least take the lantern, Miss Trelawny.' He held it out.

'And light myself up to be seen? I thank you, but no. I found my way here in the dark and I will find my way back as easily.'

Cate moved away, resisting the urge to look behind her. The town was in darkness, doors and shutters closed, only occasional strips of yellow light showing through warped timbers. When she reached the Ancle Posada and lifted the door latch, she breathed a sigh of relief, then realised she had failed to search for Lovett's ship. No matter, it would not leave harbour at night and she could look for it in the morning.

Back in her room, Cate was restless and paced the floorboards. The smiling face of Henry, and the evil faces of Elphick and Lovett, swam in and out of focus. This night was so long!

Slowly her heart beat returned to normal, but the incident of the sea-wall had sharpened her thoughts. She had little time left before the Spanish Princess sailed again. She wanted to see Lovett's body hanging from a gibbet for the sport of crows!

Cate shuddered, ashamed at such base thoughts. The man's death would be sufficient. But she could not wait for the Royal Navy to catch him. He was within her grasp.

Yet now that the moment was near, she hesitated. She wondered what her father would have wanted her to do. He had been an honourable man and an eye for an eye was not his belief. But she couldn't just let Lovett get away with his crime!

'Oh, what to do.' *Tomorrow I will be stronger*, she told herself. *Tonight I am too tired.*

Cate slipped between the cool sheets. She laid her head on the pillow and stared at the ceiling. Slowly she recovered her resolve. She would follow her original intention in honour of her father — find Lovett and take his life. Exhausted, she closed her eyes, and at last fell into a deep sleep.

5

Henry woke with a start at the sound of a door closing softly on the floor below. He sat up in the narrow bed and listened, but there was no further sound. It wasn't yet dawn. If the sound was from Cate's room, she had been out late.

He propped his pillow against the wall, leaned back on it and allowed his thoughts to drift again to Cate, the image of her holding his hands and twirling round, her hair flying out around her head, and laughing. He smiled in the darkness.

Then he sighed. Cate hated him. Or rather, she hated the man she knew as Lovett. He didn't know what he had done to bring about this reaction. Then she had asked for his help in finding Lovett and, having not revealed his full name earlier, he could not now simply bring it into conversation.

What was he to do?

The cry of gulls broke into his thoughts. Henry saw a faint light had spread across the ceiling. Throwing off the sheet, he crossed the room and pulled back the curtains. The horizon had lightened to a pale blue. There should be a fair wind for sailing. It would be hard to leave Azul, but he must go.

As he pulled on his shirt and breeches, a bell began the call to Matins. Almost six. Pulling on his boots, he strode towards the harbour to inspect the Oceanus.

Despite the early hour, there was bustle on the quay. Ships readying to sail, their flags snapping in the breeze, sailors running to and fro, carrying loads. Henry crossed the plank onto the Oceanus and called to a man working on his vessel.

'Are repairs progressing well?'

'Aye, sir. She'll be ready soon enough.'

Henry inspected the work to the hull, then climbed down the ladder. In the galley a metal box of fresh sand had been set, ready for the fire. He lifted the lid of a barrel and looked inside; beef had been laid down and salted. Bags bulging with hard biscuits and dried peas sat tidily in the corner. The entire ship would be scrubbed and gleaming before they set sail on the morrow.

He retraced his steps to the Ancle Posada, to eat breakfast ... and perhaps see Cate.

★ ★ ★

At first light Cate stirred, gradually remembering what she intended to do. In an instant she was fully awake. Her fingers trembled slightly as she washed and dressed in her working clothes. She had no appetite for breakfast and no wish to let Abella know her plan, so she hurried from the inn.

The town was bustling with sailors and storekeepers about their business before the full heat of the day. Dried salted fish swayed on strings, mixing with the scent of the sea. Cate hastened to the harbour, lively with ships in the fresh morning air. Exotic figureheads from Spain, Venice and the Orient danced on the water. She felt the familiar eagerness to get back to the sea. But first she must search along the quay. Few pirate ships had their names painted on, so she looked for a sloop with a hole in its hull. Was Elphick's information correct and the ship here?

'Cap'n! Ma'am!'

Through the clamour on the quay, Cate recognised Morgan's cry. He hailed her from the deck of the Spanish Princess. She weaved through the throng of swaggering pig-tailed men, and store-owners hurrying out with sail cloth and victuals hoping to make a sale to those from the newly-arrived ships. She reached the Spanish Princess's mooring and called up to Morgan. 'How goes the work?'

'We'll be ready to sail with the morrow's wind.'

Would that be long enough? She fervently hoped so. 'Very good. Are supplies on board?'

'Aye, the dried stuffs. The fresh will be loaded this afternoon.'

'Then there will be nothing to keep us here.' *Nothing except what I have set out to do*, she thought.

Morgan touched his cap. 'If that's all, Cap'n.'

Cate waved a friendly dismissal and he disappeared from sight. She remained on the quay and considered the ships. One of these must be Lovett's. She strolled along, examining each sloop as she passed.

Elphick emerged from the doorway of a tobacco store, stepping into her path. She came to a halt. 'Miss Trelawny.' His smile didn't reach his eyes. 'You are up early. You have suffered no ill effects from last night's unfortunate experience?'

'As you pointed out, men are not infrequently found in their cups at night by the harbour.'

'Well, let us talk of other things. I had hoped to be here before you, in order that I might have news of Lovett's ship before I renewed your delightful acquaintance.'

'I decided to look for him myself.'

'If I may?' He held out his arm.

'Don't let me detain you, sir.' She moved forward, making him step aside.

'You do not, Miss Trelawny.'

He matched his pace to hers and they strolled along the harbour wall. Cate was all too aware that they must look to anyone's eyes like two people content in each other's company.

* * *

Henry rounded the corner of the shore road. Cate's back was to him, but he recognised her immediately and his stomach turned in pleasure. He was about to hurry forward, when he realised the man whose company she seemed to be enjoying was his chief mate. Henry didn't know Elphick well — he had joined his ship only a few months ago, when Henry's old chief mate retired.

He watched the pair stroll along, admiring the ships. A small boy playing tag with his friends ran unseeing into Elphick's back. The man turned sharply to remonstrate and his eyes met Henry's. A startled look flashed across Elphick's face. He lowered his head towards Cate and said something to her, before drawing her away from the quay and down a footpath leading to the church.

Henry scratched his chin. The look on Elphick's face. Did the man seem ... afraid? But why? Henry had imposed no prohibition against acquaintance with women when on shore.

It was not surprising that Elphick should find Cate attractive, but he was surprised she enjoyed his company. They had turned towards the church. Matins would be over, but perhaps they wished for religious contemplation.

In which case he would not disturb them.

Repairs on Oceanus were progressing and they were soon to depart Azul. Henry decided to continue to the chandlery to examine sail-cloth.

If he missed Cate when she came out of church, he'd make sure he saw her this evening at Abella's.

★ ★ ★

98

'What is the hurry, sir?' Cate was not happy to have been steered away so abruptly from examining the ships. She drew to a halt on the church path.

'We must be careful not to arouse suspicion,' said Elphick, glancing behind him. 'I have heard that Lovett is a brutal man.'

'I am not afraid of Lovett.'

'Be assured that I will fnd out exactly where he is. But first, madam, pray tell me what is your intention when I have located him?'

'I have not yet decided,' she said. It was none of his business. The sun had been steadily rising and the air was becoming hotter by the minute. 'I came out without a hat, sir, so I will return to the inn.'

'Of course.'

'But, Mr Elphick, please let me know if you hear further news of Lovett.'

Cate made her way back to the Ancle Posada. She was not concerned about the sun — she was used to life in the open air — but she had no desire to stay in Elphick's company any longer than was necessary.

* * *

Cate and Abella had finished a midday meal of bread, cheese and olives when Elphick arrived. Abella reluctantly showed him into the room where they had been eating and stood in the doorway, her arms folded. She glared at him. 'Your visits are becoming somewhat frequent, Mr Elphick.'

A flash of anger kindled his pale eyes. 'I think Miss Trelawny will be pleased to hear what I have to tell her.'

'You have news?' said Cate.

He flashed Abella a sly smile, before turning to Cate. 'Lovett's ship, the Oceanus, is moored at the far end of the harbour.'

Oceanus, the Greek god of wonderful strength, with the upper body of a muscular man and the lower body of a serpent. Not to be treated lightly.

'If there is nothing else, then I thank you,' Cate said, rising.

'My pleasure.' He bowed. 'Perhaps we will meet again before I sail?'

'*Perhaps.*' *But not if I can help it*, she

thought.

Abella stood aside for Elphick. With a last glance at Cate, he left the room. Abella slammed the door behind him.

'I am going out, Abella,' said Cate.

'Not until that man is well away from here.'

'If I'm not back for supper, please don't worry about me.'

'Of course I will worry about you!' cried Abella. 'What in the name of the Blessed Mary do you think I'm going to do? You are like a daughter to me and I want to know what you intend to do.'

Cate paused. This was her own pursuit and she had to deal with the consequences. 'It is better if you don't know, Abella.'

'This is madness, Cate. Please, let it go. You cannot bring your father back.'

Cate shook her head. 'I need to do this, else it will overshadow my life.' Tears came to Cate's eyes and she took a shaky breath. 'I'm sorry, dear friend, but now is the time.'

She brushed past Abella, wrenched

open the door and ran upstairs. She hesitated only for a moment, before she slid her hand under the mattress and pulled out her knife. Easing it out of its sheath, she pressed the tip of the blade against her thumb until a drop of bright red appeared. 'Blood for blood, father,' she whispered.

Sucking the wound on her thumb, Cate returned the knife to its sheath and pushed it into the leather belt round her waist. She tied a blue bandana around her head and tucked in every curl. She gave one long look around the room as if it might be her last sight of this dear place. Then she let herself out of the inn, and into the heat and silence of the afternoon siesta.

Cate slipped down to the harbour, passing houses and shops shuttered and quiet. She'd told Abella the truth. She could not live with herself if she let Lovett slip out of her hands and away to sea.

Ships bobbed in the water, their hulls bumping gently against the dockside, their lines creaking. The smell of sawn timber and hot tar from ship repairs was almost overpowering as she walked along the quay. At the far end of the harbour, a little further along where she and Elphick had walked that morning, she found the sloop.

She wanted to get this over with, so that she would no longer be plagued by the name Lovett. When this was done, she would be free to see Henry Darley again.

Keeping close to the walls of the shops and houses, taking advantages of the few shadows, Cate crept nearer to the vessel. A movement on the sloop caught her eye. She put her hand to the hilt of her knife and was reassured by its cold, hard surface. Two men languidly played cards on the deck of the Oceanus.

Was their captain there, taking a siesta in his cabin? When Cate had seen him, standing in the prow those few days ago, he'd been a shadowy figure. She had no clear picture of his face.

The sun beat down on the quay and

the images shimmered in the heat. It was such a beautiful day to deal with such an ugly action, but it had to be done. Cate stepped forward and called up to the two men on deck. 'Where can I find your captain?' She shielded her eyes from the sun.

The men came forward and bent over the rail, looking down at her. One of them whistled appreciatively. 'Sure, and we've got a young lady here dressed up as a laddie.' He grinned, showing blackened teeth.

'Now, what would such a lovely lady as yourself be wanting with the Cap'n?' said the other.

'I know where he is, miss,' said a childish voice at her side.

Cate turned and saw standing next to her a young boy. He pointed towards the stores lining the harbour. 'Captain went in the victual store.'

Ignoring fresh catcalls from the two men, Cate crossed the cobblestones towards the shop. It was the only one in the process of opening up after the siesta.

Otherwise, the street was quiet.

She stopped at the open doorway and peered inside. Sunlight filtered hazily through the half-closed shutters onto sacks and barrels arranged on the floor. The place smelled enticingly of spices and tobacco. She saw no one, but felt again for the knife at her waist and slipped in through the low doorway.

Cate stood, waiting for her eyes to adjust to the dim interior. Now she could see there was a customer. Standing with his back to her, a tall, slim man wearing a long doublet and a dark bandana was examining the merchandise in one of the barrels. Her heart thudded. Sweat trickled down her back. Lovett. It must be. She took deep, silent breaths to steady herself and looked around. The store owner was nowhere to be seen. Never again would she have such an opportunity.

Cate wiped the sweat from her eyes. She stole forward, her light footsteps making no sound on the sand-covered floor. She drew her knife. Her mouth was dry, as she tightened her hold on its hilt and raised her trembling arm.

'Lovett,' she said in a small, cold voice.

The man spun round and grasped her wrist. She twisted and tried to pull away, but he pressed hard and she felt her fingers weakening. She looked up into his face. Cate stared in horror and her knife fell to the floor.

'Catherina,' said Henry Darley.

6

Henry saw Cate flush to the roots of her hair. 'I thought you were Lovett.' She shook her head. 'Please, let go of me.'

He stared incredulously at her. 'Why on earth would you want to kill him?' He released her wrist, picked up her knife and pushed it next to his own in the sheath at his hip.

'That is my knife, sir,' she said, biting her lip in what looked like an attempt to hold back tears. 'I would be more comfortable if I keep it for now. I think it's time you and I had a talk. Outside.'

The door at the back of the shop opened and a man in a rough sacking apron entered. He looked from Henry to Cate. 'Can I help you, señor, señorita?'

'I will be back later for my purchases,' said Henry. 'I cannot speak for the lady.'

He took hold of Cate by her elbow and guided her outside. Back in the brilliant sunshine, she allowed him to lead her into the tavern next door, sleepy and empty in the afternoon heat.

Henry called for strong black coffee for them both. He waited until Cate had swallowed some of the bitter liquid and then he spoke.

'Now, tell me what is going on.'

'I'm very sorry,' she said. 'It was never my intention to harm *you*.'

'It certainly didn't seem like that.'

'I didn't mean to harm you,' she stressed, pulling off her bandana. Her face was hot under his steady look. He knew she hadn't intended to kill him, Darley, but it was clear she wished Lovett dead. 'What are you going to do?' she asked.

'I haven't decided yet,' he said. 'First, tell me about you and Lovett.'

'There is no me and Lovett,' said Cate.

'Well, something is clearly amiss,' said Henry. He folded his arms, leaned back in the chair and stretched out his long legs. 'You'd better tell me what Lovett has done to you, before you get yourself hurt.'

Cate stared at the coffee grains in the bottom of her cup. She set it down and met his eyes.

'I can defend myself — '

'God help me, woman, the only reason I didn't cut your throat with my own knife is because I thought you were a lad sent to do a man's work.' His voice softened. 'Catherina, tell me, please.'

'My father was John Trelawny,' she blurted out. 'Our family has lived for generations in Pentreath Castle in Cornwall. My father was a gentleman and a ... maritime merchant, of sorts. We were happy despite the untimely death of my mother — until the day he was brought home fatally wounded from an ambush at sea.' Her voice faltered. 'The last thing he said to me as he lay dying was a name — Lovett.' She raised her face to Henry. 'You see why I must find this man Lovett? My father came home to tell me the name of his killer.'

Henry felt the blood drain from his face. This was why she hated him?

But he had not been responsible and

could not think why her father had named him.

'Mr Darley,' said Cate, shocked. 'What is it?'

'I know you are the daughter of John Trelawny. I recognised you when we met. It was wrong of me not to say so earlier.'

'You know me!' cried Cate, starting. 'You knew my father?'

He rubbed his brow. 'No, I didn't know John Trelawny. I met him but once. My father and he were acquaintances.'

'Acquaintances? But how so? You told me you are from Dorchester. That must be many miles from Cornwall.'

'It is some one hundred and fifty miles.'

'Then how did our fathers know each other?'

'Some business interest initially, but it moved on to friendship. I believe from time to time they met in Plymouth, convenient for both of them.'

'Plymouth! How did you recognise me? I have never been to that town.'

'Your father paid a visit to my father at our estate in Dorchester, some twelve years ago, and he brought you with him. How could I ever forget the funny little girl with long black curls?' He smiled at Cate, but she frowned.

'If our fathers were known to one another, why is your name not familiar to me?'

'My father died six years ago. You would have been still young then.' Henry paused. Now he must tell her. 'There may be another reason for your not knowing my name. I told you it is Darley. That is true, I am Henry Darley. That is my family name. But I also have another name.'

'What do you mean?'

'I am also known as the Earl of Lovett.'

'Lovett?' She blinked. 'So you are a relation of the pirate Lovett who killed my father?'

He grimaced. 'I am the pirate Henry Lovett — but I swear that I did not kill your father.'

Cate leapt up from her seat. 'You lie!'

'Madam, I do not,' said Henry, his look grim.

'I don't believe you!' Her hand flew to

her waist. 'Oh, where is my knife?'

'I have it,' said Henry, his voice soft. 'You cannot expect me to return it to you in your present state.'

'Give me my knife, sir.'

'I cannot, Catherina.'

Cate glared at him. 'You kill my father, lie to me, steal from me —'

'Come, I have just told you that I am not responsible for your father's death, and that is not a lie. I will return your knife once you have calmed down.'

Cate lunged for her weapon sheathed at his hip, but Henry was quicker. In one smooth movement, he caught her, turned her round and pulled her onto his lap.

'This is much better state of affairs, Miss Trelawny, to discuss —'

Cate stuck her finger in his eye, he let out a yell and raised a hand to his face.

She bounded up off his knee, turned and bolted out of the tavern door.

Through his one clear eye, Henry saw her glorious dark curls bouncing as she rang.

Cate flew into the Ancle Posada and straight into Abella. Abella squealed and dropped the tankards she was collecting from the tables.

'So you are back for supper, after all,' said Abella. 'I am very relieved.'

'Oh, Abella!' Cate stood trembling.

Abella took Cate into her arms. 'What is it?'

'I've seen him,' gasped Cate. 'Just now. Him.'

'Whom, child?'

Abella held Cate away from her. Her face dropped at the dishevelled state of the young woman. 'Lovett? Is it Lovett of whom you speak?'

'I've not only seen him,' she said, her voice cracking, 'I've spoken to him.'

'Tell me!' Abella stroked tendrils of hair back from Cate's eyes. 'Do you mean Lovett?'

'Yes ... no ... '

'I don't understand.'

A sailor entered the inn and dropped

into a chair. 'Abella,' he called, 'bring me a cup of rum and some of your fine stew, there's a good woman.' Other men pushed through the doorway behind him.

'The supper crowd are early,' murmured Abella to Cate. She called out, 'Just you be patient.' She lowered her voice. 'Cate, go to my parlour and wait there. I'll join you as soon as I can.'

In Abella's room, Cate threw herself onto the sofa. The reality of what she had tried to do made her feel sick. She had attempted to kill an innocent man. Cate pinched the bridge of her nose. But no, not innocent. Lovett and Mr Darley were the same person. Yet Mr Darley was kind and charming and Lovett was a monster. She put down her head and sobbed.

Before long Abella burst into the parlour and pulled up a chair. 'Now, my dear, tell me everything.'

'Oh, Abella. I don't know what I have done. Mr Darley has shown only kindness towards me, but just now I went to attack him with my knife.' She drew a shaky breath.

'You attacked Mr Darley with a knife?' Abella looked startled.

Cate took a deep breath and began again. 'I went down to the harbour and found the ship Elphick had told me about. Lovett's sloop, the Oceanus. I was told the captain was in the victual store. It was dark inside because the shutters were closed, but I saw one customer. The man was standing with his back to me. I crept up behind him, pulled out my knife and ... '

'Mother of God!' Abella crossed herself.

'Before I could strike, he turned — and it was Mr Darley.'

'You tried to kill the wrong man?'

'No, the right man,' said Cate. 'Mr Darley and Lovett are one and the same.'

'He has been using a false name?'

'Not really,' said Cate. 'Henry Darley is also the Earl of Lovett.'

'Saints preserve us! I have an Earl staying here and you try to kill him?'

Cate suppressed a bitter laugh. 'I didn't succeed in avenging my father.'

'Thanks be to Mary,' said Abella. 'How could you have been so foolish, child?'

'I told you I was going to do it!'

'But you cannot be sure this man is the guilty one,' Abella said, exasperated. A thought struck her. 'What did Mr Darley say about your father's death? He was still able to speak?'

'Yes.' Cate gave a shaky laugh. 'I left him alive and well, unfortunately — or fortunately — I cannot tell which. He denied it, of course. But he would, wouldn't he?'

'But, Cate, he would say the same if he were an innocent man. I never should have said anything to you about this.' Abella put her head in her hands.

'Do not distress yourself, my friend. What I did this afternoon was of my own volition. Indeed, Elphick has told me more about Lovett than have you, and you at least tried to dissuade me.'

'I think we both need a drink.' Abella rose and took down from a shelf a bottle of rum and two cups. She poured out the rich liquid and handed one cup to Cate. 'Drink this.'

Cate took it thankfully. She drank too quickly and coughed, tears coming to her eyes. 'Oh, what a state of affairs, Abella.' She wiped away the tears with the back of her hand and gave a rueful smile, adding, 'And he is still in possession of my knife.'

★   ★   ★

'It is possible, mi amiga,' said Abella, pouring oil into a pan a short time later, 'that we have mistaken Mr Darley.' She corrected herself. 'I mean, the Earl of Lovett.'

'Lovett will do.' At the kitchen table Cate took a large red pepper and sliced it open. 'I liked Mr Darley,' she said, her voice softening. 'How could he have tricked me so?'

'But he told you his name in all honesty. He didn't know you blamed him — or Lovett — for your father's death.'

'When I told him Lovett had done my father a serious wrong, he didn't tell me his full name.'

'But what if Lovett is innocent?' Abella persisted, turning to Cate. 'That would mean another is to blame.'

'But who? And why?' Cate frowned. She put down the knife.

'It's difficult to understand why anyone would have wanted to kill your father. I remember him only as a kind and courteous man.'

'But someone meant to kill him and on his death-bed he named Lovett. What else can that mean?' Cate snatched up the knife again and grabbed another pepper.

'I don't know, child.' Abella shook her head in frustration. 'But somehow I feel Mr Lovett is an honest man. Unlike . . . '

'Unlike?' Cate looked at her friend.

'The other man, Elphick.' Abella took a second knife and began slicing onions. 'I do not like the way he behaves with my serving maid. She can handle the common seamen flirting with her, but there is something unpleasant about that man.'

'I don't like him, either.' Cate cut open another pepper and scraped away the seeds.

'You met him for the first time yesterday and within hours he comes to you with information on Lovett,' said Abella.

'I know.' Cate picked up a half of the pepper and bit into it.

'Elphick or Darley. Clearly, one of those two men is not to be trusted. You need to work out which one.'

'Maybe neither can be trusted.'

Abella gathered up the vegetables and tossed them into the sizzling pan.

'Don't let the whole business turn you into a simpleton. Think with your head as well as with your heart.'

Cate rose and kissed Abella on the cheek. 'I know you always have my best interests at heart, for which I thank you.'

'Go on now,' said Abella, blushing with pleasure, 'let me get on with preparing supper.'

Cate mounted the stairs to her room and sat on the edge of the bed. When she thought of Mr Darley's handsome face, it was with pleasure; when she considered Lovett, her emotion was anger. How could she have these two contradictory feelings? It was surely impossible.

At the knock on her door, Cate froze. Could it be Mr Darley? Surely not after what had happened.

She slipped off the bed and with care turned the door handle.

The face of Morgan appeared and she sighed in relief. 'Ma'am,' he said, 'The repairs to the Spanish Princess are complete and the men await instructions for sailing.'

At once Cate knew what to do.

'Thank you, Morgan. I have some business to attend to here. If I am not back by ten of the harbour clock in the morning, you must take command and sail her safely back to England.'

'Captain?' He frowned.

'Those are my instructions,' she said, her voice firm. 'I know I can place my ship in your capable hands.'

'But ma'am — '

'Mr Morgan,' Cate said, softening her voice, 'I have known you all my life. Please believe me that there is something I must do.'

Before he could say anything else, she pushed him out of the door, closed it and waited there until at last his heavy footsteps receded.

Cate scrambled through her belongings and founded a scrap of paper and a pencil.

Dearest Abella, she wrote. *I am so sorry that I must leave in a hurry.* She wrote on, thanking her friend for all her kindness and begging her not to think badly of what she was about to do. Cate folded the letter, placed it on the dresser and left a pile of coins to cover her bed and board.

Once again she forced her curls into the blue bandana. Taking only the clasp-knife from her bag, she left, closing the door softly behind her.

The moon shone white on the furled sails of the ships as Cate moved stealthily across the deserted harbour. She reached the Oceanus and glanced around the quay. All was still. Taking a deep breath, she jumped at the thick rope securing the ship to the dock. Gripping it with both hands and wrapping her feet about it, she hung for a moment, catching her breath. She moved along the rope until she reached the hull, eased herself over the side and landed with a soft thud on the moon-lit deck.

Cate waited, slowly letting out her breath. There came only the sounds of snoring.

Half-a-dozen men lay spread-eagled on rugs in the sultry night, their mouths open in deep sleep. Another fellow, slumped on rope coiled in the corner, stirred. The Midwatch, Cate guessed. Midnight to four in the morning was a hard time to stay awake. The Oceanus moved gently in the water, as if anxious to slip its moorings and be back on the open sea.

She crept along the edge of the deck towards the stern, keeping to the shadows. She was confident with the layout of the sloop, as it was of the same order as the Spanish Princess. Before she reached the ladder down to the captain's cabin, Henry Darley mounted the deck. No, she corrected herself, Henry Lovett.

She ducked down behind the water barrel. That black hat trimmed with a red feather, the long coat, the swagger. Had Henry Darley ever really existed? She reached for her claspknife, her hand tightening on the handle.

There came muted voices. Lovett was talking to another man she could not see, but it was a voice she recognised and her chest tightened.

Elphick. What was he doing here? He'd said he was a sailor — but on the Oceanus? She could make out only the rise and fall of conversation. Elphick was clearly on good terms with Lovett. Where they in league together?

Elphick crossed the deck to the pirate sleeping on the coiled rope and kicked him hard. 'Wake up, man!'

The other man's eyes shot open and he struggled to his feet. 'Aye, Mr Elphick.'

He straightened his jacket and tried to look alert.

Cate didn't hesitate. Taking advantage of the distraction, she edged across to the ladder and down to the captain's cabin, opened the door and slipped inside. With fortune in her favour, she would accomplish the deed and steal unnoticed off the ship, return to the Ancle Posada and in the morning re-join the Spanish Princess for home.

For such a wicked man, Lovett's cabin was clean and tidy, with a polished table, softly-lit by the lamp, and it held an intoxicating, musky scent. She must concentrate. First, search for any evidence ...

Books on a shelf: the Bible, poetry, medicine. He was a man of intellect and sensitivity. A dresser: on top lay a quadrant, compass, ship's log, writing materials. She opened the dresser door and peered inside ... clean clothes in a neat pile, shaving brush, bag of coins ... what was this? Something small and hard wrapped inside a white linen square.

Cate lifted it out and peeled back the cloth. Her mouth dropped open.

A signet ring. Gold with a black onyx in the centre. Her fingers trembled as she lifted the ring. Yes, there was the inscription. She stared at the ring in dismay while her legs threatened to give way and the tears ran. With a shaky sigh, she dashed them away. All at once she felt weary beyond belief.

Wrapping the ring again in the handkerchief, she slid it into the pocket of her pantaloons.

Cate sank to the floor, her back against the hard bulkhead, clasping the knife. She focused on the cabin door. But as time passed, her eyelids grew heavy and her heartbeat slow and steady. In the warmth of the cabin her eyes started to close . . .

★ ★ ★

Cate jerked awake to the heavy rattle of a chain. Her heart missed a beat. The anchor was being raised and she was in

Lovett's cabin. Worse, the flame in the oil lamp no longer burned and a pre-dawn light filtered in through the portholes.

A bump, a creek, the men calling to each other and the ship started to move. Cate scrambled to her feet, and without thinking ran to the door and wrenched it open. There came a shout from above and she looked up to see the scowling face of a pirate staring down at her. 'Oi, you, boy!'

She slammed the door shut. Snatching up the wooden chair, she wedged it under the latch. She felt for her knife, but it must have slipped from her grasp as she slept. There was no time to search.

The porthole.

Cate ran to it and pushed it open. She could swim back to land; it wasn't far. She pulled herself up and pushed her head and shoulder through the opening. The door crashed open and the chair flew across the room. The pirate snarled, crossed the cabin in a moment, grabbed her hips and pulled. She kicked back at him.

'Oh no, you don't!' He gave a hard tug and she fell to the floor.

Cate rolled onto her back. He raised his boot to kick her. She caught his foot and he fell on top of her. She pushed him off and with horror saw light dawning in his eyes. As she struggled, her bandana slipped off.

He sat back. 'Not a boy at all!' He grinned.

Sweetly, she smiled at him. His grin widened. She raised herself to her feet slowly and leapt at him, scratching his face and eyes. The pirate let out an oath. Cate kicked his shin and bounded up the ladder. She burst onto the deck and all faces turned towards her. In the ghostly light of early morning, there were two familiar, but not welcome, faces.

Henry recovered and a dark look passed across his face. 'What is the meaning of this?'

His words were addressed to the pirate who had stumbled up the steps after her and was now standing on the deck, breathing hard. Raucous laughter burst from the other men at the sight.

'She's no match for you!' called one pirate.

The injured man looked sheepish. 'I found her inside your cabin, Cap'n. And this ...'

He held out the claspknife Cate had dropped.

Henry took it from him. 'Dear me,' he murmured, 'Another weapon.'

He addressed the man. 'On with your duties. And keep away from the lady. That applies to all of you,' he bellowed, looking round the deck at his bemused men. 'Fail to treat her with respect and there will be dire consequences.'

Relieved to hear those words, Cate could only stand and wait, her heart sinking, as the coastline of Azul grew smaller.

Henry turned to her. 'Now, Miss Trelawny, tell me what the devil you are doing here.'

7

Abella was already in a state of alarm, having found that morning the note Cate had left for her. When Abella's brother appeared at the inn shortly after breakfast, she was at first astounded and then furious with him.

'You saw her last night at the harbour? What was she doing? Why did you not stop her?'

'Why would I do that?' said Alberto. 'Any bacon left for breakfast?' 'Never mind that. Tell me everything.' She folded her arms and glared at him.

Casting a longing look at the empty pan on the stove, he said, 'I was sitting at the harbour, watching the ships for a while before turning in. After a while I noticed Cate making her way along. When she got to the sloop that came in with the cannon ball hole in the hull, she stopped and looked around. I didn't see her after that. I think I was dozing under the influence of your excellent rum.' He smiled at the memory.

Abella banged the table with her palm. He jumped and his eyes flew open. 'Get on with the story,' she hissed.

'Maybe she climbed aboard the sloop.' He scratched his cheek. 'The mooring is empty, so it must have sailed this morning.'

Abella groaned. 'I'm going to see how I can help my friend,' she said, untying the cloth round her waist and throwing it on the table.

Leaving Alberto gazing towards the frying pan, Abella hurried down to the harbour. She had to find Morgan. He'd been with the Spanish Princess since John Trelawny owned it and Abella knew him well enough. She discovered Morgan in agitated conversation on the quay side with some of his crew and she hastened towards him. His face was creased with anxiety.

'Mr Morgan,' she said, 'can I speak to you privately on an urgent matter?'

'Mistress Abella.' Morgan dismissed the men.

She frowned. 'You're sailing? But — '

'Do you know where Cate is?' he said.

'No — that's what I came to ask you. Surely you won't sail without her?'

'She told me to take the Spanish Princess back to Cornwall if she didn't appear by ten o'clock.'

'It's exactly as I feared!' Abella put a hand to her forehead.

'If you know what she's about, tell me quickly,' he said. 'All of us are concerned for our captain.'

Sailors and fishermen bustled about their business.

Abella lowered her voice. 'This morning I found a note from Cate telling me she was going to deal with Lovett. My brother saw her last night looking at the sloop with the repaired hull.'

'She'd traced the man?'

'Yes. And when I think about her foolhardy behaviour yesterday — '

'What did she do?'

'She tried to kill him!'

Morgan's face hardened. 'Foolish girl. I should have seen it coming, knowing her — and knowing what he did.'

'I don't know what he did!' cried Abella. 'None of us do.'

'Her father accused the man with his own dying breath.'

'From what Cate told me, I don't believe John Trelawny said any such thing.'

'He died with the man's name on his lips,' said Morgan, stiffening. 'I heard him myself.'

'Oh, this is useless.' Abella turned away.

Morgan grabbed her arm. 'Wait, Mistress. Perhaps Cate did not board Oceanus and is still in Azul.'

She turned back. 'She boarded it, I'm sure.'

'So this is the business she referred to,' said Morgan, releasing Abella's arm. 'Our captain is set on revenge.'

★ ★ ★

Henry turned to his chief mate. 'Mr Elphick, kindly escort Miss Trelawny back to my cabin and see that she is made comfortable. I will be down directly.'

Elphick nodded and in silence led her down to Lovett's cabin.

She felt humiliated, like a child awaiting punishment for some foolish action and unable to act. Fury simmered inside her — fury with herself, with Henry Lovett and with Elphick.

As soon as Elphick ushered her inside the captain's cabin, Cate rounded on him. 'Mr Elphick, you deceived me.' He merely inclined his head. 'Why did you not tell me you were of this ship when I asked you about Lovett?'

He held her gaze. 'I had my reasons.'

'Did Lovett send you to spy on me?' Cate demanded.

He frowned. 'Why would you think that?'

'Because we met on too many occasions to be a coincidence.'

Elphick gave a short laugh. 'My presence in each of those places had nothing to do with Captain Lovett, I assure you.'

The door closed and she was shut in the cabin once more. She stood in the middle of the floor, furious with herself for being caught in this impossible situation.

She paced the cabin, thinking hard. The Oceanus was now too far from shore to swim, launching a small boat would attract attention and Henry Lovett would not have had her returned to the cabin if a weapon were stored there.

Cate sank into a chair at the map-strewn table. With a lift of pleasure, she realised they were sailing home to the south-west coast of England. She thought of the Spanish Princess, sailing home under Morgan's control, and prayed she would again see her ship, her crew and her home in Cornwall.

There came quick footsteps down the ladder and she rose to her feet as the door opened.

'Miss Trelawny.' Henry Lovett entered.

The cabin boy followed, carrying a tray with a coffee pot and mug. When the boy had put down the tray and left, Henry said, 'I didn't expect to meet you again quite so soon.'

'I have no wish to be here,' said Cate coldly.

'May I remind you that I did not give orders to have you seized and brought onto my ship.'

He was right, of course. She had boarded the Oceanus without his permission or knowledge.

'I did not think you of all people would be a stowaway,' he continued.

'I did not stow away!' As if she, a captain of her own ship, would stow away anywhere, least of all on his ship.

He poured out a mug of coffee. 'Then it seems you have been spying on my ship.'

Again she was stung to anger. 'Spying! Good God, what an accusation.'

'Then what are you doing here?' He slid the steaming mug across the table towards her.

'I came on board to ... to talk to you.' He raised an eyebrow. Cate held his look. 'I have many questions.'

'You could have asked me these questions yesterday. It would have been less painful than having my eye gouged.'

She thought she saw a smile play around his mouth. 'A gentleman would not have pulled me onto his knee!'

He lowered himself into the chair Cate had vacated. 'Ask away. We have plenty of time. Perhaps four weeks to reach England.'

'Four weeks!' She knew how long the sailing took, but the thought of being trapped on board for so long with this man was unbearable.

'Please consider yourself my guest.' He went on looking at her as he stretched back in his chair.

'Is this how you treat a guest — taking the only seat?'

'You can sit on my lap again, if you wish.' He smiled slowly.

She flushed. 'I do not.'

'Or there is my bed in the corner.' His smile broadened.

'For goodness' sake!'

'You are a difficult guest to please.'

'I am a most unwilling guest, as you know.'

'I'm afraid that cannot be helped. You are on my ship and we are sailing. Would you prefer to be cast overboard or deposited on the first island we see?'

Cate suppressed a shudder. There were a number of uninhabited islands in these waters and she had no wish to be abandoned on any one of them.

'You wish to consign me to certain death?' she asked.

'Isn't that what you wish for me?' Cate's mouth fell open and he gave a short laugh. He leaned forward. 'Come, Miss Trelawny. Let us not argue about this. We are forced into each other's company for some weeks, like it or not. Now, are there any other questions?'

'I haven't even started yet.'

'My humble apologies, I thought you had.' He rose and perched on the edge of the desk, indicating that she should take his seat.

'I find I prefer it here, after all,' she snipped.

He rose. Picking her up, he carried her to the chair and set her down in it. 'That is better,' he said, resuming his seat on the desk.

She pushed the chair back and pulled his folded handkerchief from her pocket.

He frowned. 'What have you there? Have you searched my cupboard?'

She opened the snowy folds. 'Is this yours?' On her open palm she held out the ring.

'No, I found it.'

How he could lie! 'And where did you find it?'

He folded his arms. 'It was among the possessions of one of my crew.'

'Then bring him here,' she said, closing her fingers round the ring.

'I cannot,' he said, his face grave.

'Because he doesn't exist?'

'Because he is dead. Killed during the battle between your ship and mine.'

She breathed deeply. 'How did he come to have my father's ring?'

'I have no idea.'

'Oh, you deny knowledge of everything — '

'I am telling the truth, Miss Trelawny.

I found the ring in his pocket and placed it in my cupboard until I can give it to his widow.'

'Look inside the band and you will see my father's initials. JT.' She held out the ring.

He took it and tilted it towards the light. 'I can see the initials as you describe.' He looked at Cate. 'I am inclined to believe you.' He took her hand and placed the ring in her palm. 'Do you have any more questions?'

'Only one, for now. What happens when we get back to England?'

'You will be free to go.' He looked down at her. 'But you must promise not try to kill me again.'

Cate hesitated. If she agreed, her quest for revenge would be over. If she did not agree, then what? She had no choice. She lifted her chin. 'I accept your demand.'

'Good.' Henry looked at her shirt and pantaloons. 'You cannot wear the same clothes until we reach England, although you do not appear to be the sort of female who cares much for her appearance.'

'That is ungallant, sir.'

'My apologies. It was a mere observation.'

'I do require a change of clothes ... '
Her bag was still in the Ancle Posada and the remainder of her belongings on board the Spanish Princess.

'I will find you something. I'm sure the ship's boy will have clothes to fit you. You appear to be the same sort of shape.'

What an abominable creature he is, she thought. How could I ever believed him otherwise?

★　★　★

Cate Trelawny really was a surprising young woman, thought Henry. Such a mix of bravery and foolhardy behaviour he had not encountered before. This journey should be an interesting one. Henry leaned back in his chair. The adorable Cate he'd met on Azul was not the same person as this angry young woman. During these weeks together on the Oceanus, he would take the opportunity to get to know her and to persuade her of his innocence.

He'd instructed Elphick to vacate his cabin for Miss Trelawny. Elphick would sleep in a hammock below deck, as did the rest of the crew.

Henry turned his attention to the trunk of clothes in the corner of his cabin. He did not really expect Cate to wear the clothes of a ship's boy. Ah, but she had looked beautiful in the pale yellow dress at the gathering. He hadn't spoken the truth just now about her lack of womanly curves. The loose breeches she wore could not disguise her sweetly-rounded derriere. If only he had a gown to give her. He imagined her walking towards him ... The delicious image dissolved. His men would try to gain her attention and fights would break out. She should continue to wear the simple clothing of a pirate.

Henry grinned. His own clothes would swamp her, so that is what he would give her. Opening the trunk, he rummaged inside until he found the necessary garments. He added a short length of cotton fabric. He closed the lid and gathered up the pile. Carrying them to Elphick's cabin, ignoring the ribald cries of his crew, he knocked on the door.

'Who is it?' called Cate.

'Henry.'

She opened the door. 'Yes?'

He held out the garments. 'I have found a few things for you to wear. You may wish to make from the cotton those, um, delicate garments which you lack.'

Cate gathered the small pile into her arms. 'You trust me with scissors?' she asked, the corners of her mouth lifting involuntarily.

He smiled. 'I believe I am safe now. Would you like me to send hot water to wash?'

'Please,' said Cate and closed the door firmly.

★　★　★

The Oceanus sailed steadily on with the wind at her back. Cate had dressed in the clean garments given to her by Henry

142

Lovett. They were far too large, and she had a suspicion they were his and that had deliberately chosen such clothes, and she suppressed a laugh.

She leaned on the rail, looking out to sea. Her damp hair would soon dry in the warm afternoon breeze. She hadn't been prevented from leaving the cabin and so far had been treated well. In truth, he was not as she imagined a pirate to be. Yet always her mind came back to her father speaking Lovett's name. Morgan had been on the Spanish Princess when it was attacked. He swore the man had singled out her father as his target, but he had not seen the assailant's face.

Closing her eyes, she felt the way he had tenderly tucked a curl behind her ear after the gathering. She imagined being held against his powerful frame, his masculine warmth. Her eyes flew open. She could not fall in love with Henry Darley while hating Lovett!

She startled as Henry appeared beside her, and placed his strong brown hand near hers on the rail. He smiled at her

and there was something in that movement of his lips that made her glance
away, a faint heat rising in her cheeks, to
look instead at the glittering Mediterranean.

'The garments suit you,' he said
simply.

She turned towards him. 'I had to
use my belt, as you see, and roll up the
sleeves of the shirt and the legs of the
pantaloons. But otherwise, yes, they fit.'

'That wasn't quite what I said, Miss
Trelawny.' A beat or two of silence passed
between them. 'I think we need to talk
... Don't you agree?'

'We must.' She lowered her lashes,
afraid he would see the confusion in her
eyes.

'Let us have dinner together this
evening. Will you join me up here later?'

Cate nodded and Henry moved away,
but she continued to stand there, tast-
ing the salty sea breeze on her lips. She
had been on Azul with her ship ready to
sail home, and now she was at the mercy
of the man who had been her enemy for

half a year. Her life kept turning upside down.

For the remainder of the afternoon Cate stayed on deck, savouring the wind in her hair. She kept her distance from the men as they worked or played cards, and she sent angry glances at Elphick every time he looked in her direction.

Everything about her future seemed uncertain.

Before she returned to her cabin in the early evening, she wondered if Oceanus himself looked down on her. If he did, she thought, he would see a small figure helpless on a toy ship sailing on the vast open sea.

★   ★   ★

As night fell over the Mediterranean, Henry dressed with care in his black frock coat and a clean shirt. When he returned on deck, a small table had been set up as he'd requested and laid with a white tablecloth and silver cutlery. Two crystal wine glasses sparkled in the light of a lantern that swayed from the rigging. The usual sounds of the ship had quietened, as the men had retired below to eat and to sleep.

Henry watched Cate walk towards him, her hips swaying in the way he loved so well. He rose from the table and pulled out the chair for her.

'Thank you,' she murmured, her expression unreadable in the shadows cast by the lantern. The cook brought the food on porcelain plates and returned below deck. 'This is kind of you.'

'I like to dine on deck when I get the chance,' said Henry. 'Usually I am too busy to eat anywhere but in my cabin.'

'And you are not too busy this evening?'

'No.' He smiled. He wanted nothing this evening than to be here, with her.

The fried chicken was delicious. For a while the sound of the dark sea washing against the hull provided the only accompaniment to the meal.

Cate dabbed her mouth with the linen napkin, Henry laid down his cutlery and raised his glass.

146

'To what shall we drink?' he asked.

She didn't hesitate. 'Honesty.'

He let the words fall into the silence between them and echoed the toast. 'To honesty.'

She drank a little of the white wine and put down the glass. She tilted her head back to look at the heavens and in doing so exposed her neck. He was sure he could see a small pulse throbbing in her throat, as if it were begging for kisses.

Henry tore his eyes away and up to follow her gaze. Above them were layers and layers of stars, almost unbearably beautiful in the darkness. It was a night for romance. He wished things could be different, but there was a conversation they must have.

He set his glass down on the table. 'A lady should speak first.'

She drew her eyes down and toyed with the stem of her glass. 'It is difficult to know where to start,' she said at last.

'At the beginning is invariably the best.'

She gave a small smile. 'I have told

you my father was John Trelawny.' Cate took a sip from her glass. 'My father and I had always been very close, and this bond was strengthened on the death of my mother. I accompanied him on as many of his sea voyages as he would permit. I wanted to be with him, I loved the sea, and he was happy to teach me everything he knew.'

Cate paused as Henry poured her a little more wine into her glass.

'We sailed as privateers. My father was a good man and he never deliberately harmed a living soul. Sometimes in skirmishes one of his crew would be badly injured, or killed, and my father would be heart-broken. He knew and cared for each of his men and their families as if they were his own. No widow or child was ever put off our land if their man died while sailing with him or working his land.' She glanced up at Henry.

Used now to the shadowy darkness, he could see her features. His steady look did not stray from her face as she continued.

'That last time, my father refused to let me come. I knew there was something different this time. He said only that it was more dangerous than usual. When the Spanish Princess returned to Pentreath, I saw him carried, mortally wounded, into the castle. He spoke only one word before he died. Lovett.' Cate bit back tears.

Henry stretched forward and reached a hand towards hers, but she pulled away. In a shaking voice, she continued.

'Later, when I could think more clearly, I asked his chief mate to tell me what had happened. Morgan said the Spanish Princess had been given instructions by the Crown to sail to the French coast, wait for a particular French vessel, seize the special cargo it carried and bring it back to England. But she was ambushed as she waited in the bay and some of our men lost their lives.'

'Did the French ship not give chase?'

'No. One of our crew had disabled her and she could not sail after us.' Cate passed a hand over her forehead. 'Once the Spanish Princess was safely away, my father was found to be badly wounded from a single sword thrust. The ship's doctor was injured, so Morgan did his best for him, but my father lapsed in and out of consciousness during the days it took to reach home. When he was back at Pentreath, he rallied briefly, but only to utter your name before he died in my arms.'

Henry stirred at her obvious distress. What could he do, or say, to help?

She finished her wine in one gulp and pushed the glass away. 'So you see,' she said, her brows furrowed, 'What do you expect me to think, other than that you were responsible for his death? Morgan said he heard a man on the other ship shout out in English, although their captain screamed in French for the boarding party to attack. You are an Englishman who speaks French; you did so at the gathering on Azul.' Cate bowed her head. She looked so very tired.

'Only a little French, remember.'

'And now,' she said, 'I want to hear

what you have to say on the matter.'

'I am sorry you think me capable of such despicable behaviour, but truly I am not the man who killed your father.'

'You must admit that everything points to you — your name on my father's lips, his ring — '

Henry pushed away his chair, rose and leaned against the rail, shadows around him.

'Very well, it is my turn now. I met John Trelawny only once, when I was a youth and you a child, as I told you earlier. Other than that, I heard my father speak of him and I know that they respected each other and corresponded over a number of years, until my father's death.

'As to the day you describe,' Henry continued, 'I cannot say what happened because I was not there.' Henry pushed himself from the rail, moved back to the table and resumed his seat.

Cate said slowly, 'So you don't know why my father's ship was attacked in this way?'

He shook his head. 'I don't know the truth of the matter. Mr Elphick has told me ... But that is idle gossip.'

'Elphick! How is he involved?'

Henry frowned. 'He told me he'd heard that it was the Spanish Princess which attacked and boarded the French ship, and that John Trelawny's fatal injury was a part of the skirmish.'

Cate pushed back her seat. 'He is lying!'

'But tell me,' said Henry calmly, 'is it not more likely that your father, in attempting to take the prize, ambushed the French ship?'

She shook her head. 'My crew would have told me. No, Elphick conceals the truth.'

'But why would he?'

'I don't know! Of course it is right that you trust your chief mate, but it is his account, based on gossip, against my entire crew.'

Henry inclined his head in acknowledgement. Since Elphick had joined his ship, the man had not socialised with any of the crew. On a ship, living and working together for weeks or months at a time, it was essential there was harmony. His men did not like Elphick and, if Henry were honest, he was not sure that he did either.

He looked at Cate thoughtfully.

'I want to believe you,' she said, distressed. 'I have been consumed by revenge for so long. I just want it to be over.'

'Then let it be,' said Henry, his voice gentle. He reached out his hand and this time she took it. He felt her fingers tremble slightly in his clasp.

'This means,' she said with a small sigh, 'that the true killer is still out there.'

'Then we must find him.'

'We?'

'If you will allow me.'

She gave a nod that was barely perceptible. 'What of the special cargo? None of my father's crew saw it.'

'I don't know, but I will find out. And now,' said Henry, his voice full of concern, 'You look so tired. We have talked enough for this evening. Let me take you back to the cabin.' She was suddenly shivering. 'You are cold, Miss Trelawny. Allow me.' He slipped off his long jacket and drew it around her shoulders, fighting the longing to hold her close to his warm body. 'The air is changing,' he said. 'I fear a storm is on its way.'

8

Cate woke to the shimmering light of dawn. Her thoughts came flooding back and all at once she could not bear the confinement of the cabin. On deck, a breeze ruffled her hair, but it did not soothe her and her heart didn't match the gay mood of the Oceanus as it cut through the waves, the men whistling as they went about their work.

The Spanish Princess must also be on her way home, captained by Morgan. Once back in Cornwall, perhaps her life would continue as before, as if none of this had happened. Was that what she wanted? She suppressed a sigh. Now that she believed that Henry was innocent, there were even more questions than answers.

'You're an early riser,' said Henry's deep voice, startling her out of her thoughts.

He stood a whisper's breath away and in his eyes she read a sensual message. She turned to scan the horizon, to hide the effect he had on her. The sea stretched out with no land in sight. Ominously, the air temperature had dropped, the breeze had changed direction, growing stronger.

'A captain has to rise early,' she said. 'Do not forget that I am one.'

'You must miss your own ship.'

'I do.'

'You will be back home before too long,' he said. 'The Spanish Princess cannot be far behind and you will be able to take charge of her again. Isn't that what you want?'

'Yes.' She bit her lip and he raised an eyebrow. 'Things have not turned out as I expected during this voyage,' she said, her voice hesitant.

'And what did you expect?' Henry asked.

'Some sort of resolution.'

'You may yet have one. There are many possibilities to the outcome of a journey.'

The wind quickened and the Oceanus rose on a wave. Henry slid a steadying arm around her waist. She was taken off guard by the warmth of his body against hers.

'Cate,' he murmured. He tilted her chin up and brushed his lips against hers, sending her pulse racing. He raised his head and said nothing, but kept his arm around her. She had a sudden desire to lean her head against his chest, to feel that strength, that certainty.

Instead, unsure of herself, she pulled back and said, 'Was that appropriate, sir?'

'Most definitely,' he said with a grin. 'But let me give you something by way of apology for my wanton behaviour.' His long fingers reached up and lifted a fine gold chain from around his neck. He slipped it over her head and the beat of her heart quickened. She stood for a long moment without moving, afraid to break the spell, then her fingertips traced the fine links of the chain against her throat.

'You are impossible, sir,' she said. 'You take liberties, and then bribe me and expect me to thank you.'

'The chain is a gift I want you to have.'

'Why?'

'It looks better on you than on me.' He smiled.

She shook her head, sure he was teasing her, and moved to take off the necklace, but he held out his hand to stop her.

'I wish you to keep it.'

'Then, I thank you,' she said.

'I know you did not intend us to be forced together like this, but it has happened and I am not sorry.' The teasing was gone. His eyes were dark with desire. He leaned so close that his lips were almost touching hers. Her breathing quickened, her heart raced. Again he brushed his lips against hers.

He stepped away. 'I cannot kiss you as I would wish, in full view of my crew.'

'They are too busy to notice.' She grinned, feeling daring.

'Ah,' said Henry, 'but a pleasure postponed is a pleasure increased.'

Cate felt the pulse of disappointment. She wanted to feel his arms tight about her.

'A storm is approaching,' he said, indicating the darkening horizon.

'I had noticed the signs.' Cate smiled impishly. 'I am an experienced sailor, you know.'

'I know, to my chagrin,' he said, but the twitch of his lips betrayed his words. She laughed. 'But for now,' he said, 'I would feel happier with you safely in your cabin.' He bent down and kissed the tip of her nose.

'Perhaps,' she said, 'But I would feel happier if I had some say in the way we approach the coming storm.'

'Very well. What is your preferred method?'

'Either make for the open sea, away from the path of the storm, or heave-to.'

'I think we should heave-to.'

'Aye, aye, Captain,' she said with mock seriousness.

She watched as he gave orders to trim the main sail in hard and lash the helm. Thunder rumbled in the distance.

Soon lightning flashed overhead and

with it came crashing thunder. Before long, rain beat down on the deck and the ship rocked violently.

Henry came to her side and took her in his arms. 'It is not safe. Please go to your cabin.'

She raised her head, saw his grim look and nodded. His warm lips brushed her cold ones, and she turned her away from him. Hanging onto the rail, she made her way on the heaving ship towards the ladder.

It was hot in the cabin and dark as the rain coursed down the portholes. Her mind whirled and pitched with the waves, as she thought of Henry and his crew battling on deck, and of her own ship with her men on the same sea.

After what felt like hours, the rain gradually stopped, but through the port-hole the sky remained slate-coloured, the wind continued to rise and waves buffeted against the hull. Gradually a numbness came over her, until in spite of herself she was lulled to sleep.

★ ★ ★

When Cate awoke the night was black. She raised herself up from the bed. Something was wrong. The ship was still tossing about in the waves — but the men were shouting frantically and someone was calling her name. She struggled to her feet, felt along the wall and pulled open the door. A bolt of lightning lit up the sky and thunder rumbled across the water. She snatched up Elphick's cap and cape and tumbled out the door.

Scrambling up the ladder, she emerged onto the darkened, clamorous deck as a sudden wave dashed over her. The shock of the cold and wet was like a knife in her lungs. There was roaring and shouting, and objects were sliding around her on the deck. Drenched and cold, she clung to the rail to stop herself being swept out to sea, and looked for Henry. When her vision cleared and her breath returned, she spotted him in soaking shirt and breeches battling at the helm.

'Henry!' she screamed.

He turned sharply towards her. There came a loud cracking sound over the clap of thunder.

'Look out!' Henry yelled.

Cate looked up as the mast snapped. She stifled a scream as it crashed to the deck. Men howled as they were knocked overboard and there came the dreadful cries of another crushed by the fallen mast.

Rigging and sails lay in a tangled mess everywhere. The wet cape lashed her body, her soaked breeches stuck to her legs and strands of hair from under the cap whipped across her face. She stumbled across the pitching ship and called above the wind. 'She will break up!'

'It's too late to save the ship,' Henry shouted, his features hard. 'We're too many crew down.'

The deck was awash and the ship listed dangerously. She saw Elphick lose his footing on the wet boards and fall backwards. His mouth opened in a piercing scream and he slipped over the rail.

'Oh God,' she whispered.

'Everyone to the boats!' yelled Henry. He pushed the soaked hair back from his face. 'We have to abandon ship.'

She had seen one of the small boats carried away by the waves and another smashed to matchwood against the side of the ship. There could be only one boat left.

Henry pointed into the wild night. 'The storm is taking us towards shore. See the lights? There must be a harbour there and we can take shelter.'

'It could be Barbary pirates,' she shouted above the storm.

'Wreckers? We'll have to take that chance.' He raised his voice to be heard above the roar of the waves. 'We don't have a choice, Cate. If we don't put in there, we'll crack up on the rocks.'

'Can't we stay at sea until the storm dies?'

Mountainous seas heaved and rolled, the sky as dark as the water.

'We won't ride it out!'

The remaining boat was being launched, men stumbling along the deck towards it.

'Get in the boat,' Henry ordered.

'Not without you,' she screamed.

He let out an exasperated groan, abandoned the helm and scooped her up. He carried her to the rail and tossed her to the waiting men in the boat; they reached up and caught her. The sea tossed the little boat up and down, as she stared up at the rail.

Henry jumped, disappearing into the dark sea. For a moment there was nothing, then his head broke through the surface of the water and he struck out for the small boat. The men pulled him in, he moved over to a spare oar, tucked his sword behind him and they began to row.

Cate counted the men silhouetted against the horizon. The ship's boy, Thomas, with his shoulder wound not yet healed, the ship's doctor, the carpenter. Only four. Lightning flashed across the sky and Cate saw the carpenter had blood running down his head. All had ghastly faces in the eerie light.

The boy pointed. 'There's Mr Elphick!'

Weaving around the floating planks and bobbing casks on the water, Elphick swam towards them. His head kept going under, but his face was intent on survival each time he came up. Henry hauled him in, laid him face down and thumped his back. Elphick coughed.

'That's it, man. Get it up,' said Henry.

'Captain,' said the boy, 'Look!' Henry turned back to the stricken vessel. 'She's going down.'

Cate followed his gaze and as if in a bad dream saw the proud Oceanus lying on her side. Sea poured over the deck, the rudder banged to and fro, the ship groaned. Barrels rolled out of the hold on a surge of water and floated away.

'Pull,' shouted Henry, and they pulled for all they were worth.

Cate's eyes were smarting with seawater and as she blinked them clear, she prayed that the Spanish Princess and her men would survive this dreadful night!

In front of them the dark cliffs of the unknown coast rose nearer and nearer, while the lights nestling below promised safety.

At last they were close to the island, but then the little boat juddered and she heard the crack of splintering wood. A cry rose from the men above the crashing of the sea. 'We've struck a rock!'

'Jump!' Henry shouted. 'Every man for himself.' He grabbed Cate's hand.

She looked at him desperately. 'I'm not a good enough swimmer for this sea.'

'Hold tight.' He squeezed her hand. 'Jump with me.'

Quickly he unfastened the cape from around her neck and hand in hand they leaped into the swirling water. The sea rose over the top of Cate's head and the shock took her breath away. She swallowed a great gulp of salt water and felt herself being pulled, gasping and choking, to the surface. Henry's face appeared within inches of hers, his hand holding hers tightly. A strong wave broke over them again and her hand was snatched out of his grasp.

'Cate!'

She heard him call her name, but the wave lifted and carried her further away from him. She tried to raise her head to breathe air, not water, and was tossed around in the sea, half-swimming, half-drowning. There came another wave, so fierce it lifted her bodily and flung her onto a rock. The air was forced from her lungs.

She clung to the rock as the wave swept over her again, enveloping her in its coldness, and drained away, trying to suck her back with it. Her hold on the rock loosened. Gasping, she climbed higher and then she was over the top and onto the sand. With what remained of her fast-ebbing strength, she dragged herself up the beach, crawling further from the reach of the sea. She slid into a sandy hollow and the world went dark.

★ ★ ★

Washed onto the dark beach, Henry lay unmoving. He came gradually to his senses, but lay for a moment, his limbs and body aching. He pushed himself up into a sitting position and cast about for Cate. Where was she? Painfully, he got to his feet and searched desperately around.

The night sky was cloudy, obscuring the moon, but he could make out bodies floating in the sea. No, some were not dead but were struggling to reach shore. *Let one of them be Cate*, he prayed.

He plunged back into the angry sea, reached the closest of the swimmers and dragged him to shore. His cabin boy was still breathing, although his energy was spent, each breath sounding weak and painful. Henry left him to rest on the sand, waded back in and dragged a second man from the water. He lowered him onto the beach and saw it was Elphick. The man's breathing was heavy, his grasp on life strong. Henry turned to the sea again, scanning the dark water. No one else was visible; all had disappeared under the waves. 'God save their souls,' he murmured.

Had one been Cate? He mustn't allow himself to think that. He would search the beach. She was a fighter.

'Captain.' The voice was Elphick's. Henry spun round and saw his chief mate had pulled himself up against a rock. 'You saved my life,' croaked Elphick.

Henry squatted down in front of him. 'How are you feeling?'

'Where's Catherina Trelawny?'

Henry shook his head. 'I don't know. Stay here and rest, I must find her.' He rose and stepped forward. A hand reached out and grabbed his ankle. Henry went flying, his hands and face hitting the sand, knocking out his breath. Elphick scrambled to his feet. As Henry began to climb to his, a boot pressed into the back of his neck.

'I can't allow that.' The boot pressed harder. 'She deserves to die.'

Henry rolled onto his back, caught Elphick's foot with both hands and jerked it up, sending the man sprawling onto the sand. Henry sprang up, wrenched his sword from its sheath and held against Elphick's throat. 'How dare you!'

'Don't think I haven't noticed how

you look at each other.'

'What's it to do with you?' Henry pressed the point of his blade against Elphick's skin.

Elphick coughed. 'If you want me to explain, slacken your sword.' Slowly Henry lowered the blade. Elphick pulled himself into a seated position. 'You have no idea?' he sneered.

Henry flicked his sword point at Elphick. 'Speak, man.'

Elphick scowled. 'I knew her father, John Trelawny. The first time I met the man was when my son got work as his ship's boy. You didn't know I had a son, did you?' Henry shook his head. 'Jacob couldn't wait to go to sea. He begged me to let him to sign up. I'll never forget the day I took him to the harbour to say goodbye. He was excited to see so many ships, the bustle at the piers, the open sea.'

Henry leaned against a rock to steady himself, keeping a watchful eye on Elphick.

'The second time I met Trelawny was

when he came to my house to tell me Jacob was dead. There'd been a battle with an enemy ship and my sweet, innocent boy had been killed.'

'I am sorry for that,' said Henry. 'It must be sad to lose a child.'

'Sad?' said Elphick, his reddened eyes blazing. 'It was devastating! Jacob was our only child. My wife never got over the shock.' His breaths came in angry gasps. 'We ran a tavern in Plymouth, a nice little business, but when our boy died — ' He broke off, unable to continue.

'You must have known it's a dangerous life and that risks come with it,' said Henry carefully. 'It was good of John Trelawny to break the news to you himself.'

'He offered me money. As if money could compensate for losing Jacob.' Elphick's voice dripped venom. 'Trelawny felt guilty. He knew he should have taken greater care of my boy.'

'What does this have to do with Miss Trelawny?'

Elphick rose to his feet and pulled out his sword. 'I don't think I will tell you, after all.'

A cloud moved away from the waxing moon and the light reflected off their weapons as the two men faced each other on the beach.

'Come, man, put down your sword and we'll find a way to get you back to your wife.' If they fought, only one of them could survive this night.

The sword in Elphick's left hand glinted as it slashed towards Henry's neck. Henry raised his weapon and knocked Elphick's blade off course. For a split second he considered ducking sideways and running his sword through Elphick, but he was loath to kill him.

Their blades swished in the night air. He felt a sharp pain in his right arm as Elphick's sword cut his salty skin. The cut sharpened his senses. He would not die in this ignoble way, in a duel with his chief mate on a deserted island. If he must die young, it would be in a battle at sea as befits a pirate captain.

Cate's image flashed into his mind, smiling up at him on the sun-lit hill in Azul, laughing as they whirled round in the dance at the gathering, the warmth of her skin …

He snarled and fought on, their blades flashing, but still Elphick would not give up. Gathering his final ounce of strength, Henry slashed at Elphick's wrist. Blood spouted from the wound and the man's sword fell to the sand.

Elphick staggered and gaped down at his bloody wrist. Henry moved quickly, tearing a strip off the bottom of his shirt and binding Elphick's wound tightly. Elphick swayed, making no sound. When Henry finished the rough dressing, Elphick carefully lowered himself onto a rock with his other hand. He was silent for a moment, then his breathing steadied but his cheeks were pale.

'I asked you about Miss Trelawney,' said Henry, standing over him. 'Why is it that you would see her dead?'

'They say confession is good for the soul.' Elphick gave a weak cough. 'I met her by chance at the harbour on our first day in Azul. When she told me her name, I realised she was Trelawny's daughter. As I watched her walk away, it came to me what to do. I followed her at a distance, then waited on the cliff top.'

'To do what?' said Henry, his voice low.

'It's a quiet spot, there would be a chance there. But that half-wit Alberto came along.'

'A chance?' repeated Henry, tightening the hold on his sword hilt.

'Then I saw her on the sea-wall that same night, just before an old sot attacked her. That made me laugh — here was someone who could swing for her murder instead of me — but dammit she was too clever for him and the fool fell in the drink.' He paused to draw breath. 'By that time, there'd been too much noise and I couldn't risk doing the job myself.' He gave a short laugh. 'Cate Trelawny had to be charmed.'

'Whereas you are the very devil.' Henry clenched his jaw.

Elphick's words were coming slowly and a little slurred. 'She thinks you killed her father.'

'I know,' said Henry, grimly. And then all at once he knew what Elphick was going to say.

Elphick fixed his eyes on Henry. 'I killed him.'

He stared at Elphick's face, ghastly in the moonlight. Cate had blamed him, Henry, for her father's death and from that had followed her hatred of him, the attempt on his life, her hiding on his ship . . .

'It would have been better if you'd admitted it earlier,' said Henry.

Elphick managed a painful shrug. 'John Trelawny ruined my life. He was responsible for the death of my boy — and of my wife.' Henry winced. 'Oh yes, it got worse.' Elphick coughed. 'After Trelawny brought us the news, my wife lost her mind. She couldn't sleep or eat, and she wandered the streets day and night. The tavern suffered, for I needed her to help me run it. One evening, when I was downstairs working in the tap room, she swallowed poison. By the time I found her, it was too late.'

'Dear God,' said Henry. 'Such a dreadful way to end one's life.'

'So you can see why I had to kill John Trelawny. The business failed and I was forced to give up the tenancy. But I didn't care any longer. I had nothing left to live for.' He paused to ease the position of his bloody wrist. 'I took any work, slept rough, wandered until I reached London, got a job on a ship and finally found myself in the crew on that French merchant vessel. Coming upon the Spanish Princess and John Trelawny was simply a lucky chance and I seized it.'

'You were my chief mate,' said Henry. 'How you have deceived me!'

Elphick's eyes had grown dim. Henry doubted the man would last the night. 'And Miss Trelawny?' He had to know.

'When I realised who she was, I didn't see why she should keep her life. The death of Trelawny for that of my son and the death of his daughter for that of my wife.'

'You killed John Trelawny in cold blood and you would have done the same to his daughter.'

Elphick's voice was faint. 'You may as well know about the special cargo, too ... '

Henry had to lean forward to hear what he said. He caught a few words. Before he could ask another question, Elphick's eyes closed and he slid sideways off the rock onto the beach.

Exhausted now, Henry staggered over to where the boy still lay. He checked his pulse, but it was too late. A desperate sadness seeped into him as he closed the boy's eyes. He dragged himself to his feet and stumbled along the sand, calling for Cate, but his legs gave way. He sank to his knees and lost consciousness.

9

Cate slowly opened her eyes and blinked. The sun was high in the sky, she was dazzled and her eyes stung from the salt water. She looked about her and whimpered softly. She was lying in a sandy hollow. For a moment she wondered where she was, and her heart sank as she remembered. Feeling bruised and sick from the sea water she had swallowed, she sat up carefully.

The storm had passed over. The sky was now clear, but the sea remained violent and dark green. Her clothes had dried in the sun, but her hair was gritty with sand, her curls hung about her face in matted locks, she was barefoot and her skin smarted.

Cate crawled out of the hollow, her shirt and breeches stiff with salt, and sank down onto her knees. The smell of cooked fish hit her nostrils and her stomach clenched.

Some feet away a group of men crouched around a camp fire on the beach. Her spirits lifted — it must be Henry and his men! She opened her mouth to call to them, but her throat was dry and sore and no sound came.

She struggled to her feet. With a jolt she realised they were not Henry's crew. Everything about their wild appearance, from their shaggy hair to the ragged and colourful clothes they wore, told her they were Barbary pirates. She glanced around for a rock to hide behind, but it was too late. She'd been spotted. The man stood and pointed in her direction, speaking to the others. They all turned to stare at her, slow sneering grins appearing on each of their faces.

Despite the intense heat of the morning, Cate shivered. Her hand slid towards her knife, but it wasn't there. Henry had taken it from her days ago. She pulled back her shoulders, lifted her chin and waited.

A tall, heavy man with a long black beard and a tricorn hat atop wild hair broke from the group. His emerald green tunic, though richly embroidered in gold thread, was grubby — unlike the cutlass hanging from the belt at his waist. She guessed he must be their captain. The man sauntered over to where she stood, as if challenging her to run. Her pulse thumped in her ears as he drew near. A livid scar ran across his forehead.

'Los saludos,' he said, letting his eyes travel down her until at length he looked up and spoke in English. 'A pretty wench.'

'Who dares to address me so?'

'I like a girl with spirit.' He made a grab for her.

She lifted her hand to slap his away, but he caught it in his roughened grasp. 'You'd best be nice to me,' he said, a scowl passing across his face. He dropped her hand and, pulling off his hat, bowed so low that his greasy hair swept the sand. 'Solomon Green, at yer service.'

For a moment Cate could not remember where she had heard the name. Then it came back. He was the corsair captain Abella had mentioned. Cate tried to speak but it came out as a cough.

''Tis a pity we can't offer you any food at present, for it's all eaten, but there's liquid refreshment.' He flicked a finger at one of the men round the fire and made a tipping motion towards his mouth. The captain's fingernails were black and broken, but on the middle finger of his right hand glittered a large emerald.

The pirate jumped up, brought over a leather flask and held it out to Cate. Over his shoulder, she saw the corsairs' ship at anchor.

She took the flask, pulled out the cork stopper and rinsed her mouth. Rum, of course. She spat it out, close to the feet of Green, watching him as she did so. He glanced down at the patch of liquid already drying in the sand and smirked. Cate took another gulp, this time swallowing it. She managed to speak. 'I believe I have heard of you,' she said, surprised that she was able to keep her voice steady. She pushed the flask back to Green. 'Have you seen anyone else from my ship? Where is Captain Lovett?'

'Don't know, but I 'spect he's dead. They're all dead, most likely.'

'No.' Her legs could not support her and she sank to the sand. 'He can't be.' She buried her face in her hands.

'Don't you fret.' Green laid a heavy hand on her shoulder. She shook it off and rose slowly to her feet.

'I'm the only survivor?'

'Ain't you a lucky woman.'

How could she think of herself as lucky? Henry was gone, and his crew. With a wrenching sob, the tears spilled out, running down her cheeks. Green was watching her with open interest.

'You speak English like a Londoner,' said Cate at last, wiping the tears from her face.

He smiled, stained brown teeth showing through his bushy black beard. 'Born and bred in Poplar, educated at the Honourable East India Company shipyard. And who do I 'ave the 'onour of addressing?'

'I am Miss Catherina Trelawny. Of Cornwall.'

'Well, Miss Catherina Trelawny of Cornwall,' he said in a thoughtful voice, 'The question is, does your papa 'ave money?'

She did not answer, nor did she allow any change in her facial expression. If he intended to hold her to ransom, it was better that the man didn't know she no longer had a father.

'Tell me,' he continued with a leer, 'What's a lovely young lady like yerself doing on a ship full of men?'

She thought quickly. 'I was sailing under Captain Lovett's protection on his merchant ship, to join my husband.'

'Yer 'usband?' Green's face fell. He glanced at her left hand. 'I don't see no marriage band.'

'We are not yet married. He is a merchant in Gibraltar. The ceremony is to take place when I reach there.'

'Ah,' said Green. 'That's good.'

The men round the fire were getting restless, their talk growing louder. Green spun round. 'Silencio!' The men looked sullen, but they fell silent. He turned back to Cate.

''pologies, ma'am. Me little foraging party here — after last night's excursions, yer know — is keen to get on. Reckon we've got as much as we can get.' He smirked.

'What is to happen to me?' she asked, unwilling to ask but knowing she must.

'Yer my prisoner, of course. But so long as you behave sensible-like, I'll look after yer. Come with me.' He held out his arm, and there were rude cat-calls and gestures from the men.

'Put out the fire,' Green called without turning behind him and he grinned at her, continuing to hold out his arm. She looked at him in distaste. Nothing could induce her to take his arm.

'I'm sure we'll deal well together,' he said.

'Indeed, no, sir, I fear we will not. And you shall not touch me.'

He grabbed her hand and pulled her towards him. 'We'll see about that. I'm sure you'll change yer mind once we're on me ship.' He pointed to the galley at anchor. 'That there's me trusty Violeta. Off you go now, good as gold.'

The men were kicking sand over the fire to put it out as she made her way over the beach towards the waiting long-boat. Green swaggered behind. As they crossed the sand, the pirate captain called out to his crew in Spanish. 'We have a real prize here, me lads. She'll bring us a high price at market.'

Market! Cate's steps slowed. She heard the men laughing and bile rose in her throat. He could only mean the slave market. They were not far from Algiers and the biggest slave auction on the Barbary coast. An awful image came to her of being deposited on the quay, chained and prodded, forced to walk through the streets to the amusement of the crowd. She'd overheard Morgan telling the cabin boy what his fate would be if he were to jump ship, that slaves for sale had to stand from early morning until the afternoon while buyers viewed them like cattle. Cate herself had heard that the ruling pasha bought most female captives and some of these were taken into his harem. From the ribald response of Green and his men, she had no doubt what they expected would be her fate.

Her heart thumped with mingled horror and fury. She was close now to the longboat. Once she was on it, escape would be much harder. Green and his men were cavorting behind her. They must be drunk. She had a chance if she took it now.

Turning, she sprinted along the sand away from the longboat. There came a torrent of abuse and the pounding of feet in pursuit. She ran fast, her naked feet and lighter body reaching a quicker pace over the sand, all the time praying that she could outrun them. But she was also weak from the near-drowning and her strength waned. There were just too many of Green's men.

One caught her round the waist and she went down with a thud. The pirate sat with a thump on her back and the air was pushed from her lungs.

Green caught up with his men now

standing around Cate and laughing. 'Bien, Matias.' He clapped the pirate on the shoulder and jerked his head to order him to get up. Released, Cate rose slowly and rubbed her sore back.

'Where did think yer were going? There ain't no escaping that way. We're on an island.' Green shook his head.

She dare not let alarm show on her face as he bundled her into the centre of the longboat. He and the other pirates jumped in, their sweat-stinking bodies too close for comfort.

As they rowed towards the Violeta, the crew stared at her with open desire. She stared straight ahead at the galley. The ship favoured by Barbary pirates had sleek lines, a necessity in a vessel built for speed. Its long slender hull glistened in the sun.

Cate cast a look behind her. She could see now that the island was rocky and doubtless uninhabited. The lights seen from the Oceanus the previous night had been a trap. The corsairs would have placed lighted lanterns around the bay, to make it look like a small village where those in peril on the ship could take shelter. She had been right, but could take no comfort from that. She bit her lip. To think that Henry had died in such a bleak place.

There was a burst of laughter and she looked up to see Green speaking to his men while they all watched her. She turned her head away, holding back tears.

The longboat reached the Violeta, and she was forced up the ladder and onto the deck. Men were rolling barrels — of water or oil she did not know — into the hold. A torn sail, two lanterns and a few boxes of hard biscuits had been laid out to dry on the deck. Spoils from the wreck of Henry's ship, she guessed. Her chest tightened.

She could do nothing but wait as Green gave the order to hoist the main-sail and his men tugged at the ropes and pulleys. The furled sails were loos-ened and each one snapped tight as the wind filled them. The ship slid forward through the water and far too soon the shore disappeared behind them. Wherever she looked she could see only water.

* * *

Henry woke to the sound of birds screaming. He sat up and squinted at the sun, his mouth parched, his head throbbing. It must be already late afternoon. He climbed to his feet, wincing at the pain in his arm where Elphick's blade had cut him. He scanned the beach, saw Elphick slumped against the rock and his ship's boy lying on the sand. Jamie was dead, he could see that.

Henry limped across the sand to Elphick and took his shoulder, but it was as he guessed. The man was dead. For a moment Henry felt sadness for the loss of yet another life, but this emotion was fleeting. Elphick had done a dreadful thing.

He looked out over the sea. It was now calm and empty. He could not — would not — accept that Cate was lying on the sea bed. He glanced up again at the burning sun and reasoned he was on the southern part of the island. To the east was a short, rock-covered beach; to the west lay a longer stretch, a mile or so, dotted with trees and white sand leading to the foaming surf.

The sun beat down and his dry lips were cracked. Picking up a pebble from the beach, he put it in his mouth and sucked on the hard smooth surface to ease his thirst. He set off along the sand, heading east. He must find Cate, and any other survivors if they were to be found.

He walked for about half a mile, as birds fished and called. At the corner of the island the rocks became more dense. There was no one here, alive or dead. He retraced his steps, sweat dripping from his forehead in the heat, and calling her name. At the sound of 'Cate!', the gulls rose as one and set up a shrieking, seeming to mimic the pain in his heart. He kept close to the shore line, moving westwards, weaving through the palm trees for shelter where possible. Small creatures scuttled into the low scrubby bushes at his approach.

A few smashed planks and ragged strips of canvas were scattered along the sands. He found a cooking pan, still on its hook and attached to a piece of broken wood. Henry wrenched the pot free and attached it to his belt.

At the end of the beach, he came to a sandy spit and just beyond, round the edge of the island, lay the wreck of a sloop. His heart rose. The Oceanus! But the next second he realised that was impossible, for he had seen his ship capsize and break into pieces. This was the wreck of another ship, one which had lain exposed to the elements for so long that it was covered with dripping seaweed. Cate had been right — corsairs used this island to lure ships and loot the wreckage.

Before Henry had time to dwell on the fate of those long-ago sailors, he almost stepped into a small stream, making its way down a rocky outcrop and into the sea. He fell to his knees at the water and, unhooking the pan from his waist, scooped it up and drank greedily.

His thirst satisfied, he rose and again scanned the horizon trembling in the haze. The corsairs had left the island. Had they found Cate and taken her with them, or was she dead? When Cate had been discovered on his ship, why did he not turn the Oceanus around and take her back to Azul where she would have been safe? 'Be honest,' he said aloud to no one but himself. 'You wanted her company, the pleasure of seeing her and talking to her every day.'

He should have told her earlier, much earlier, of his feelings. How he wanted to feel her soft curls brush against his neck, how he longed to hold her against his chest and feel her tender body tremble. He had let her slip away.

He thought, too, of his father. Deep inside, Henry hadn't forgiven himself for the distress he'd caused. A life at sea had been his boyhood wish — he'd wanted and loved that life — but now in truth he was growing tired of it. He had matured and was ready to settle down. And it was Cate he wanted to marry and spend her life at his side. But he was a pirate, a man outside the law.

The shriek of a gull penetrated the fog of regret that enveloped him. Action was needed. Cate must have been abducted by the Barbary pirates, so he would get off the island and find her. But he had another job to attend to first.

Henry returned to the bodies of Elphick and young Jamie. They had already been exposed for too long. Labouring under the blazing sun, one by one he dragged the bodies to the tree line and buried them. Their graves would be shallow, but even Elphick deserved a Christian burial. Henry said a few words over the two graves and made the sign of the cross.

His thoughts now were steady and purposeful. He must make a fire to attract the attention of any passing ship and must find food to stay alive.

There was a plentiful supply of drinking water by the spit of land, so he would make camp there. He trudged along the beach, gathering driftwood for the fire. By the stream, he laid down the kindling, felt inside his pantaloon pockets and with a sigh of relief found his tinderbox. It had not been washed away. He opened it and pulled out the small leather container, removed the damp flint, firesteel and charcloth, and spread them out on a rock to dry in the sun. He gathered pebbles to form a small firepit and placed the smaller of the dry sticks across the top.

He had no feather to act as a lure or hook to catch a fish, so he took up a piece of seaweed, tore a silver button from his shirt and threaded one end of the seaweed through the hole in the button. He waded into the warm shallows, lowered the glittery button into the sea and sat very still on a rock, holding the other end of his makeshift line, waiting for a movement in the calm water. For a while he saw only shifting white sand on the sea bed. Waves lapped against the shore and overhead came the incessant cry of gulls.

Where was Cate now and what was she doing? She was brave and resourceful, he had no doubt about that, but she was one woman against any number of corsairs. The ship must be on its way to Africa, heading for the infamous slave auctions.

There was a flash of silver scales in the clear water and the seaweed line shivered as the fish bit on the button lure. Henry jerked out a heavy bream, struck it against the rock and threw the sharp-toothed fish onto the sand.

The contents of his tinderbox were dry now. He knelt, struck the firesteel against the flint, sparks fell onto the charcloth and a small fire caught. He lifted the cloth, lit the heaped sticks and blew gently. The flame kindled. He extinguished the cloth and returned it to the container. Presently the sticks crackled and flared, and there was a small but blazing fire.

He gutted the fish with his knife, cleaned both in the sea, speared the bream onto a stick of wood and laid it across the firepit. Crouching down, he waited a few minutes until the fish began to brown, and turned it with his knife to the crackling flame. The smell came to his nostrils and his empty stomach rumbled.

As he watched the fish sizzling, his mind returned to his plans. It might be days or weeks before another ship passed and saw his signal, and there was the possibility that it might be a corsair vessel. If he could find the remains of his small boat, he might be able to make repairs using wood from the wreck of the Oceanus. He might be able to sail to another island — one which was inhabited — and find a ship and crew to take him to Algiers. Under the corsairs' noses he would snatch Cate from the market place and they would sail back to England.

He straightened his back, shook his head at the impossibility of his plan. But he'd stick with it anyway. She was heartbreakingly beautiful, but what were her feelings for him? She no longer hated him, of that he was sure, but could she come to love him?

'Oh, Cate,' he murmured, feeling the enormity of all that lay ahead.

★ ★ ★

The storm, which had lulled the morning of her capture, renewed its energy out at sea. Cate was barely aware of the time passing as her body burned in a kind of delirium. She lay in that state as night turned into day and back into night again. She tossed and turned on a bed in a small cabin, occasionally pulling herself upright to drink the water by the side of the bunk. Her dreams were vivid, more like nightmares. Henry's smiling face swam in the white and bloated features of a dead man. Each time she woke clammy and gasping, only to collapse back onto the sheet. Cate eventually sank into a deep slumber. She woke in the clear dawn, her skin cooler, her head clearer. She eased herself off the bed, her shirt and breeches stiff and reeking with sweat and sea salt, and peered through the porthole. The sea was deserted.

Still the Violeta pitched, keeping Green and his crew busy on deck. Now and again the cabin door was unlocked and a tattooed pirate set on the floor a tray with bitter coffee and small honey cakes. They settled her stomach. As she slowly regained her strength, Cate had time to think. Henry was dead. She had wanted this for so long, but now it had happened she wished it undone. She would have laughed, had it been funny.

His gold chain! She lifted her hand to her throat. The necklace was no longer there. She glanced down at her hand. Her father's signet ring was still on her thumb, so Green had not stolen that. The chain must have been washed away in the stormy sea.

She gave herself a mental shake. Henry could have survived the storm. She pictured him alive on the island and her spirits lifted. Was he catching a fish for supper, lighting a fire to cook it? She smiled at the comforting image.

Then she felt chilled. Did he think she had died? Then he would no longer be searching for her.

She knelt on the bunk and opened the port hole. The sea air flowed in, freshening the stuffy cabin.

'I'm here, Henry,' she whispered, willing the sea to carry her message to him.

Yet for now she was the prisoner of Solomon Green. She had noticed his hostile glances and the cruel twist to his lips. She shuddered, but she would not give in to fear. Showing any weakness before her captors would be a grave mistake. She needed to remain alert and make full use of any advantages at her disposal — buy she could not physically overpower the pirates, she had no weapon and was in no position to call for help.

She could hear the men laughing, no doubt delighted to be at sea again. She didn't know exactly where they were heading, only that it would be a port along the northern shores of Africa. Algiers, or perhaps Tunis. That both had slave markets was well-known. Well, she wouldn't go willingly to a slave auction — she would fight back in some way.

Presently she heard footsteps, a key rattle in the lock, and Green entered the cabin. He wore a long, faded red coat, his head was tied in a red bandana and from under it his long, greasy hair straggled down. He looked like the devil himself. He slammed the door behind him and his eye roved over her.

'I trust yer've bin comfortable while me and the lads 'ave been busy?' His teeth showed the brown ghost of a smile in the gloom.

She rose, the better to steady her resolve. 'How long have I been here?'

'Two nights.' He grinned. 'See 'ere, I've got some special clothes for you.'

She now noticed the gown over his arm, and he thrust the garment forwards. 'Feel it. 'Tis the finest taffy.'

She put out her hand and touched the crimson taffeta. The fabric was stiff and slippery and it shimmered in the afternoon light flooding through the portholes.

'Where did you get this?' The question was out of her mouth before she could stop herself. His mouth twisted into a cruel grin, and she wished she had not asked.

'Let's just say 'twas surplus to the lady's requirements.'

Cate cast her eyes towards the closed door.

'Oh-ho, don't think you can escape me.' The gleam in his eyes filled her with panic and he gave a short laugh. 'So, yer beginning to be afraid, eh? Good, I like to see that.'

She backed away from him.

'Put the garments on,' he snarled.

Green wanted her to wear something feminine and beautiful for a reason. But she glanced down at her filthy shirt and breeches and was desperate to change into something clean. She drew up the garment. A long fitted bodice which laced at the front, and skirts with a great deal of fabric at the back to enhance a lady's attributes.

He pulled a pair of Turkish silk slippers from his pocket and dropped them to the floor by her feet.

She met his challenge. 'Leave the cabin.'

He grinned. 'I call the tune.'

'Then I shan't change.'

'Yes, yer will.' He took a step towards her.

She kicked out at him but he reared back. Her foot grazed off his thigh, hard enough to make him stagger. He lunged forward with his head down and into her chest. Breathless, she hammered at his shoulders while he drove her backwards. Her back hit the bulkhead and they came to a shuddering halt.

He growled and burst into laughter. 'What spirit!' he said, 'but I ain't got time fer games.' He stepped back. 'Now git dressed.'

'Turn round,' she said, her voice haughty.

He grinned, but did as he was bid. Her legs were wobbly as she placed the garments on the bed and pulled off her own stiff and dirty ones. Keeping her eyes on him, she dropped her clothes to the floor. At the sound of their fall, Green began to turn his head.

'Turn back!' She snatched up the gown and clutched it to her bosom.

He gave a harsh laugh, but turned away again.

She quickly drew on the bodice. The fabric felt like an icy shroud. With trembling fingers, she pulled the laces together at the front, then slid the stiff silk skirts over her head and settled them on her hips, pushed her feet into the slippers.

'I am ready.' Her face burned with anger.

He faced her again. 'Turn around slowly.'

Reluctantly, Cate did so. As she turned in a slow circle, Green gave a low whistle. 'Very nice indeed. I like to see exactly what I own.'

He pulled a little ebony box from the folds of his garment, opened the lid and inserted a pinch of snuff in each nostril, all the time watching her in silence.

'Come,' he said, snapping shut the box and returning it to his pocket. He pulled open the door of the cabin and gestured for her to climb the ladder to the deck. When she reached the top, there was a sudden hush as the men stopped working and their eyes ogled her.

'Git back to yer work,' Green growled at the men as he stepped up to join her on deck. He held out his arm to Cate. 'We'll go to my cabin. It's more comfortable-like there.'

Cate ignored his arm. As she moved forward, her slipper caught on the hem of her skirts and she stumbled. A swarthy fellow with a black eye patch bounded forward to steady her and his hand brushed against her bodice. She whirled round and caught him a stunning blow on the side of his head.

'Cerdo!' Green screamed at the man, his eyes missing nothing. 'And you,' he spat at Cate, 'See that I'll discipline me own men.'

Green turned furiously to another of his crew. 'Tie this pig to the bowsprit. A dip in the ocean will cool his ardour.'

'No!' she said. 'I don't want him punished in such a barbaric way.'

'I say what goes on me own ship, missy,' he said, his lip curling. He grabbed her arm, his fingers digging into her flesh, and pulled her along the deck and into his cabin. He slammed shut the door. 'There.' He was smiling again.

At the side of the cabin was a large divan covered with red and gold silk cushions. He caught her hand and pulled her down with him onto the divan. 'Here will be best for the purpose.'

Sick, she guessed what would come next. She was thrust backwards against the cushions and his face loomed above hers. She tried to push him off but his arms pinned hers down.

'Just one little kiss, to show 'ow grateful you are for all I've done for you.'

'I owe you nothing — '

His loose wet mouth came close to her lips. She could scarcely breathe. With one fierce burst of strength, she freed her arms and pushed him back. 'Do not touch me!'

'Beg pardon, m'dear.' He stretched back in a nonchalant manner. 'You didn't like that?'

She eased herself up and glared at him.

His eyes gleamed. 'You're me spoils from the wreck of that ship.'

She was determined not to show fear, so she smoothed her skirts and spoke in a light tone. 'Pray tell me, what now?'

'You understand Spanish. I saw it when I talked to me lads about selling you at auction.'

'I am not an animal to be sold at market!'

'You're young and pretty, and I'm bettin' yer a virgin, so yer'll fetch a good price.'

'That would be a barbarous thing to do,' she said, her blood chilling.

'You think so? And what about all the Africans taken as slaves to the Americas on the English ships? Don't you think that's a barb'rous thing?'

'I do!' She thought of her father. 'I have heard that some men — naval and privateers — release any slaves they find on ships they capture.'

'Is that so?' sneered Green. 'Be that as it may,' he said, shrugging, 'yer a good prize and I'm going to sell you.' A thought struck him. 'Or I might keep yer for meself.'

Cate stared at him, striving to keep the dismay from her face. She drew away from him and he roared with laughter. There must be something she could say. 'If it's money you want,' she said, 'I am worth a large ransom. My betrothed in Gibraltar is a wealthy merchant.'

Green considered her words and shook his head. 'Even if it's true, I don't want to get mixed up in any bargains with the English. I left that cursed country long ago and don't trust 'em. To get your betrothed's money, I'd 'ave to put in at Gibraltar and that would be dangerous.'

He was right. Any pirate, corsair or otherwise, appearing there — and Green didn't look the type of man able to disguise that he was a pirate — would immediately be arrested by soldiers from the garrison.

'Then,' she said firmly, 'You must ensure I remain as pure as the auction buyer would wish.'

He sighed, stood, and straightened his tunic. 'You'd better stay in yer cabin 'til we reach Algiers. The lads haven't been in port for a while and I don't want anyone in the crew lowering yer price, if I ain't going to do it meself.'

'Algiers,' murmured Cate. Her heart sank further. 'And when are we to arrive?'

He opened the door and called for a deck hand. The corsair that arrived was tall, his face pitted with the marks of pox. The fellow took her arm and tugged her along the short passageway. As he pushed her into her cabin, a scream from above tore the air. The man tied to the bowsprit must have begun to sink beneath the waves. She flinched, but could do nothing to help him. The pirate slammed the door and locked it.

10

Henry stripped off his tattered clothes and waded into the sea. He dived and struck out away from the shore. Each day the feeling of helplessness grew and threatened to overcome him. At least the warm water soothed his body and enveloped him in a feeling of calm. When he felt he had swum far enough, he floated on his back and allowed the gentle waves to drift him back towards shore.

On the hot sand he pulled on his clothes and gathered more sticks for the fire. He stretched out on his back under the shelter of a palm tree and put one hand behind his head. In his other hand he clasped a slim gold chain.

Five days had passed since the shipwreck. He had searched the whole of the small island and not found Cate, but he had come across the charred remains of a small fire, still warm, on the sand. The wreckers had been there. Then one morning he'd been given a ray of hope. A little further along the beach from the remains of the corsairs' fire, he'd noticed something glinting in the sunlight. It had been half concealed in a sandy hollow large enough to contain a woman's slight body on that stormy night. The slim, gold chain was the one he had given to Cate. His heart gave a sudden jolt, so sharp it was physical. Cate had been here.

The sea was calm now, but the violent storm had made its mark. The Oceanus and its cargo sunk to the bottom of the sea, all his men dead. But deep in his heart, he knew Cate was alive and that thought gave him comfort. He lay now under the palm tree and his grip tightened on the slim gold chain.

The sun waned and the chill of dusk settled around him. As the last rays of daylight disappeared, absolute blackness settled again on the island. He crawled into the rough tent he'd made from pieces of torn canvas found on the beach and he fell into a troubled dream in which a sword flashed while a beautiful dark-haired woman beckoned him.

★ ★ ★

In the morning when Henry rose, he noticed the palm leaves above his head were not moving. The breeze had dropped, which meant the conditions were perfect for the fire to work as a signal to any passing ships. At last he could do something to escape from the island. He threw sticks onto the smouldering fire and when it was roaring again he tossed a handful of wet seaweed on top of the flames. The fire hissed and the column of smoke turned thick and black, rising up into the blue sky.

He scanned the horizon, but could see nothing. He took the pan to the stream for water, cooked those plants he recognised as edible, ate the flesh from a fallen coconut and gathered more driftwood to dry. Heat, hunger and constant vigilance were taking their toll, making him feel weak, but he dare not lose concentration.

The hours passed slowly as once again he watched and waited.

Towards evening, with the sun low and shadows creeping over the water, his spirits fell. Another day about to pass. As he turned from his vigil, shoulders drooping, something caught his eye out at sea. Had he sunk to hallucinations, or was that a ship low on the horizon? His heart leaped, but he forced himself to remain steady until he was certain.

Yes, a sail was now visible, silhouetted against the sky. The wind was behind the ship and Henry waited as it grew closer. He could see figures on the deck. Don't let them be corsairs, he prayed. He shaded his eyes with a hand against the setting sun to see more clearly. As he tried to make them out, poised to run back to the camp for his sword, a flag was hoisted. Henry laughed aloud, the sound strange to his ears after so long. The Spanish Princess! The ship he wished for most — Cate's ship!

He splashed through the water to his waist, waved his arms over head and gave a joyful shout. The ship seemed to fly towards him while he stood with a broad grin on his face.

Was Cate on board, having some-how escaped the clutches of the Barbary pirates? Henry watched the small boat being lowered over the side and the men rowing towards him. As soon as the first man jumped out into the shallows, Henry addressed him. 'Mr Morgan, I believe?'

'Aye,' said Morgan. Recognition, then astonishment, dawned on his weather-beaten face. 'It's surely not Mr Darley?'

'It is.' Henry ruefully rubbed his blonde-stubbled chin. 'Never have I been so glad to see a man!' He clasped Morgan's hand firmly.

'We saw your signal,' said Morgan, 'but not for the life of me did I think it would be you, sir. What has happened to bring you here?'

'It's a long story, Mr Morgan. But tell me quickly, is your captain with you?'

'No.' Morgan's face creased in con-cern. 'We were looking for the Cap'n when we spotted you. She told me to take the Spanish Princess back to England if she didn't appear. I waited for an hour after the agreed time, but she didn't come.'

'You've not seen Miss Trelawny since?' Henry pressed his lips together. 'It's as I feared.'

'What have you heard?' Morgan's brow darkened. 'Mistress Abella said Cap'n had gone aboard Lovett's ship the night before we were due to sail.'

'Let me get my few belongings and I'll tell you on board.' Henry turned towards his camp, as the men ran the small boat up onto the beach.

Morgan put a hand on his arm. 'Wait,' he said. 'If you have done anything to harm Cate — ' He moved his hand to the hilt of his sword. His men gathered round in the same threatening manner.

'Fear not, Miss Trelawny's well-being is my greatest concern,' said Henry. Seeing that Morgan and the crew had not moved, he said, 'But I fear we must sail towards Africa.'

'Africa?' Morgan tightened his grip on

his sword.

'In the storm my ship was lured onto rocks by Barbary pirates and I believe they've captured Miss Trelawny.'

'The ship our captain boarded that night was Lovett's,' said Morgan in a measured voice. 'What has that to do with you?'

'We don't have time for that now,' said Henry.

'We'll have to make time,' growled Morgan. 'Men,' he called, 'draw your swords.'

There was the swish of blades drawn from their sheaths and the glint of sunlight on the weapons.

'It's not as you think,' said Henry firmly. He saw the fierce faces and stances taken around him and sighed. 'Very well. I see I must tell you ... I am both Darley and Lovett: Henry Darley, the Earl of Lovett. But,' he added as the men stepped forward at a command from Morgan. 'I did not kill John Trelawny. You only have my word, I know, but I assure you that Cate Trelawny no longer believes me guilty of that crime.'

'Is that so?'

'We became better acquainted when she was on the Oceanus.' He reddened. 'Cate will tell you herself once we have found her. But we must get to the corsairs' ship, for I fear they intend to sell Miss Trelawny.'

'As a slave?' Morgan looked hard at him and the men waited for orders. Morgan slowly scratched his beard, then turned to the crew. 'We'll give him the benefit of the doubt, men — for the time being. I don't want to leave our captain if she's in the trouble he says.' He nodded towards the beach. 'See what you can find to eat and load it onto the ship, quick as you like.'

The men waded through the water and began an exploration of the land. Morgan followed Henry back to his camp. At the makeshift tent, Henry bent and picked up his sword and cooking pot.

'That's it? Your belongings?' said Morgan.

'All I have left from the Oceanus. And

this.' He pulled the necklace from his pocket. 'I gave it to Miss Trelawny not long before the storm broke.'

Morgan took it from Henry's open hand and examined it. 'Where did you find it?'

'Near this spot. I believe she made it onto land after the storm, but I've searched the island and cannot find her. As I said, I think she's been taken by the corsairs who lured us onto the beach.'

Morgan raised an eyebrow. 'Why weren't you also picked up?'

'We were separated in the water after the ship capsized,' said Henry. 'She must have been washed ashore here, while I was taken by the waves further along the beach.' He reached out and took back the chain from Morgan. 'The corsairs are days ahead of us. Why did it take you so long to pass this way?'

'We saw the storm coming,' said Morgan, 'and were lucky to find a sheltered bay to drop anchor until the storm passed us by.'

'Let us waste no further time.' Henry

slipped the chain into his pocket and turned towards the boat dragged up onto the beach. 'They will be heading east, to the African markets.'

Henry had an image of Cate, standing bound but holding her head high as men haggled over her price. His step faltered and he drew in a breath. 'The Barbary pirates didn't capture the Oceanus, its cargo or any of the men, as all were lost in the storm. Cate Trelawny will be a prize they'll be reluctant to part with.'

Morgan called to the crew, barely visible now in the fast-gathering darkness. 'Right men, finish your gathering. We sail eastwards.' He glanced at Henry's shirt and breeches. 'We'll find you something else to wear.'

Henry smiled ruefully at his tattered clothing. 'I wouldn't want Cate to see me like this.'

Morgan grinned. 'It sounds as though you care for our Cate.'

'It's true,' said Henry, a flush staining his cheeks. 'I have been almost out of my mind with worry about her.'

'Have no fear,' said Morgan, 'If Cate is as fond of you as you suggest, and your intentions are honourable, then that is good.'

Henry nodded, his every nerve and thought now bent upon a single purpose.

★ ★ ★

Each evening Green invited her to eat dinner with him on the deck. She loathed him, but reluctant to draw his bad temper and desperate for fresh air after hours closed up in the cabin, she accepted each invitation. The food choked her, but the wine put new life in her. It was wonderful to see and hear the lazy sea lapping against the side of the ship under the half moon.

Three days out from the coast of Africa, under the influence of wine and when he had been staring at her for some time, he burst out, 'Couldn't you be a little more agreeable?'

She looked at him with contempt.

'Couldn't you love me?' he said, words

slurred.

'Love you?' she cried. The whole situation was so absurd that she burst into laughter. 'Love you? You!'

He turned as white as the sails of the ship in the moonlight. Springing to his feet, he struck Cate with the back of his hand. The salt taste of blood came to her tongue. 'I'll make yer regret that,' he growled, wavering slightly.

Her lip stung, but she would not give him the pleasure of seeing her raise her hand to the cut.

She rose and held her head high as she returned to the cabin. Once there, she sank onto the divan and a burning flood of tears streaked down her cheeks. Thoughts of Henry, her men and her ship, their whereabouts all unknown, and of Abella who must be worried about her, had all taken their toll. Her courage had come to an end and she wept. Drained, she watched through the porthole until daylight crept over the horizon and with it came a renewal of courage. She was still alive and she would fight to stay that way.

★　★　★

The Violeta sailed on and time moved slowly. Cate was grateful that she was left alone, even though her thoughts were not happy ones. When she was allowed out of her cabin, she kept her distance from Green and the other men.

She was used to the white mist that clung to the surface of the water just before sunrise, but one afternoon a sudden change in the temperature brought a sea fog. It spread a cold dampness about them. The wind dropped and the Violeta was like a ghost, moving slowly and blindly on the sea. Cate could not see Ursa Major at night, nor the sun or horizon clearly in the day, so she did not know exactly where they were.

Her nerves were on edge, as were those of everyone else. The corsairs' songs grew ragged with drink and violent oaths flew about. When Cate left her cabin for some air, choking though it was, she could see Green pacing on deck, a thick cloak about him and his hat pulled low.

She walked on the deck for exercise and avoided the catwalk which ran almost the entire length of the galley. The oarsmen sat on benches in the pit and in the mist she could hear them rowing. Then night folded the galley and everyone in it in blackness. She knew the fog still lay on the sea by the dampness of her clothes, and seeing it on the beards of the men by the light of a single lantern glowing in the stern.

Finally, morning brought the sight she had dreaded since Green had taken her from the island, twelve long days ago. Through the porthole of her cabin, she saw land in the distance. Within hours barren brown rock became visible, broken up in patches of sandy desert with dunes that came down to the edge of the sea. The north coast of Africa.

The sun had risen and the fog vanished as quickly as it had come. Slowly the wind stirred and freshened and the sails swelled. Cate went up on deck as the ship raced through the fresh sea. Her heart began to beat faster. There was another ship on the horizon. A sloop. She gripped the rail and watched its progress. Her excitement grew as she silently prayed for rescue.

The other ship flew no colours. Could it be someone who knew of her plight? Morgan? Or Henry? She remembered the first time she had set eyes on him, standing tall on the prow of the Oceanus, his black coat blowing in the wind, and sweeping off his hat with that ridiculous feather ...

The sloop was gaining on them and some of the pirates had gathered on deck, curious to see what would happen. Green stood alert, spyglass pointed at the vessel in their wake. Cate edged towards him as close as she dared. She didn't want to draw attention to herself but she needed to hear what he intended to do.

'If he wants a fight, he's picked the wrong ship,' sneered Green to his bosun.

The sloop was fast and it was closing on the Violeta. Cate's thoughts raced. Surely it wasn't possible … Figures of men were visible on its deck, with three guns aimed at the galley. It was the Spanish Princess, she was sure.

'To arms, me lads!' Green shouted.

His men ran to and fro across the deck, calling to each other.

Green turned, saw Cate and snarled sharply, 'Git below.'

She ran down to her cabin, slammed the door behind her and peered through the porthole. With a leap of joy, she saw her colours hoisted aloft. How Morgan had learned of her predicament, she had no idea, but it was enough that he had found her at last!

Firstly, she had to let her men know she was on board. If they fired the cannon she could die on Green's ship. At least in Algiers she'd have a chance of escape, no matter how small. She looked wildly round the cabin. What would Morgan and the rest of her crew recognise as belonging to a woman?

Cate bent down and tore a wide strip off the hem of her crimson gown. She wrenched open the porthole and leaned out, waving the length of bright red taffeta until her arm ached.

More shouts from Green and his crew on deck came to her ears.

'Clear the decks for action! Gunners in position!'

Dropping the fabric on the floor of the cabin, she rang back up the ladder.

The crew of the Violeta were too busy to notice her, as they ran hither and thither obeying orders. Green was again surveying the sloop through his raised spyglass. The Spanish Princess's guns, pointed towards the Violeta, glinted in the sun.

Green lifted his megaphone and shouted, 'Fire starboard gun!'

The gunners brought their smoking embers down to the touch hole. The guns roared and slammed backwards. A boom rolled across the water. But the shots went wide and the balls skipped harmlessly across the sea.

She gave a silent prayer of thanks that the Spanish Princess had not been hit.

'Again!' screamed Green.

The men reloaded at full speed. Powder was thrown down the barrels and tamped, the balls tipped in and the wad rammed home to hold the balls in position. The gunners again aimed and fired.

This time a ball hit the sloop and the Violeta's crew set up a cheer. Cate held her breath. The cannon shot had only hit part of the deck, breaking the rail.

'Fire!' ordered Green and again the guns shouted out.

The powder smoke whipped back across the deck, stinging her eyes. She estimated that the sloop must now be less than fifty yards away as the salvos increased. The Spanish Princess did not fire back. Her men knew she was on board!

Cate inched her way round the deck until she was close to Green.

'Fire!' Cannon shots boomed out as the Violeta tried again to land a direct hit on the Spanish Princess.

How dare he! That was her ship and

her men!

As his cannons missed, Green cursed, turned towards his bosun and caught sight of Cate. 'What yer doing here? I told yer to go below!'

The bosun made a grab for her, but she ducked under his grasp and he lost his balance. She darted out of his reach as he roared at her, found his footing and went to grab her.

Green held the other man's arm. 'Leave her. We've got more important matters to attend to. She can't go far.'

The two ships were drawing slowly together, the white sails of the Spanish Princess flapping in the wind.

Cate could now clearly distinguish the figures of Morgan and the boarding party standing, pistol-armed, against the deck rail.

In the prow stood a man, tall and slim, his fair hair shining in the bright sunlight.

11

Henry's breathing quickened. Cate, his beguiling Cate, stood at the rail of the galley. For a moment he stood dazzled by such beauty among the ugliness of battle.

'Henry!' She shouted, half-laughing, raising her arms above her head. She called again, above the cries of the wounded, the frantic orders of Green and the shots. 'Henry!'

The glow in his belly spread through his body. Thank God, she was alive!

He shouted an order to the crew. 'Aim to clear their deck. Fire grapeshot on my order.' He meant to take the corsair's ship, not sink it; he could not risk Cate's life.

Henry turned back in time to see a corsair grab Cate's arms from behind and hold a pistol to her head. She struggled, but the man held her firm. Her eyes were fixed on Henry and he saw terror and longing in them. He clenched his fists in anger.

There was a short lull in the firing from the other ship. They were close enough now for Morgan to call across to them. 'Where bound?'

'Lower yer sail or we'll send yer to the bottom!' snarled Green.

'Certainly not!' shouted Henry. He turned to Morgan. 'May I take over? This is my battle, for the woman I love.'

Morgan nodded, and Henry gave the order.

'Fire!'

The gunners lit their fuses and fired a mass of small balls.

'Fire!' yelled Green and his men responded with a volley of large balls from their cannons. But the ships were too close, less than fifty yards, and the shots flew beyond the Spanish Princess. 'Dammit! Use pistols!' he roared.

Pandemonium broke out on the galley as Green's men sought to carry out his command.

His heart pounding, Henry searched

through the smoke for Cate ... She was no longer there.

Battle cries and the sharp crack of pistol shots came from the corsairs' ship.

'Fire!' shouted Henry again, and one of his cannons blazed and brought down the enemy's mizzenmast. It crashed onto the deck, debris soared into the air and an enormous wave washed over the men.

The ship righted itself, but there was panic all around, the corsairs shouting, tripping over their dead and wounded, scurrying to check damage. Henry heard Green spit out curses against the Spanish Princess, half lost in her own smoke. The corsair captain turned and screamed, 'Man the pumps, you fools!'

The mizzenmast must have cracked the stern near the waterline, thought Henry. Good. They will know they cannot fight on for much longer without the risk of their ship sinking.

'Are you ready, Mr Morgan?' said Henry.

'As ready as you are,' said Morgan.

Above the renewed sounds of shouts

and pistol shots, Henry called through his trumpet to the crew, 'Man the boarding party!'

The two ships were now so close that no small boat was needed. The men grabbed swords from the rack. Morgan and the rest of the boarding party waiting on the Spanish Princess threw grappling hooks with nets across the short expanse of water. As soon as the hooks fixed themselves over the side of the galley, Henry again raised the trumpet to his lips. From the rigging on the sloop, the rest of the crew rained shots down on the corsairs to keep them away from the netting.

'Away the boarding party!' Henry shouted.

He jumped onto the nets and scrambled across, while shots from the Spanish Princess flew above his head. Morgan and the other men followed behind, howling like triumphant demons.

As Henry reached the top of the nets, Cate pulled sharply away from the corsair holding her and darted across the deck towards Henry. She snatched up a pistol from the fingers of a man who had just fallen, a hole in his head.

Henry threw his leg over the galley's rail and sprang onto the deck. The boarding party followed and he heard the clashes and groans of men fighting hand-to-hand, as he saw the corsair captain grab Cate's arms from behind and pull them up sharply against her back. She gasped as the pistol fell from her grasp and a look of pain shot across her face.

'She don't escape me,' said Green, fixing his eyes on Henry while drawing Cate close, one hand gripping her wrists.

'Let her go,' Henry said, warning in his voice.

The sounds of the battle seemed to fade away and it was as if there were only the three of them on the ship — he, Cate and the Barbary pirate captain. Green brought his knife up to her throat. He tightened his hold on her, his eyes not moving from Henry's face.

Henry smiled without warmth and raised his voice over the screaming of combat. 'You delude yourself, whoever you are, if you think you can win this fight.'

Green pressed the blade to Cate's throat and she bit back a cry.

'You must be Cap'n Henry Lovett, back from the dead,' he said. 'I'm Cap'n Solomon Green. P'rhaps you've heard of me.'

Henry raised his right hand. His pistol shone in the sunlight.

Green gave a mirthless laugh. 'Me knife'll be faster than yer pistol, me friend.'

Henry kept his pistol raised. 'I want only one thing from you.' Keeping his eyes on Green, Henry held out his other hand to Cate.

Green sneered. 'She be worth that much to you then?'

'Indeed, so I will take this lady and withdraw.'

'And yer reckon I'm goin' to let yer do that?'

'If you wish to live it would be advisable.'

'And if I say no?'

'Then, my friend,' Henry sighed,' I'll be forced to take your ship.'

Green bellowed out a laugh.

'Consider yourself lucky,' said Henry, still pointing his pistol at Green, 'that I am not interested in taking captives. You will need those left of your able-bodied crew to man your small boats and save your miserable lives.'

'And yer expect me to agree to them terms?' said Green. 'It seems to me that I'm holding the better hand.'

'Let us fight in a manner more worthy of pirate captains. Take out your long blade and we will be evenly matched.'

Henry slipped the pistol back into his belt and felt his eyes burn with a primitive joy.

'Now why would I want to do that?'

'To prove you're not a coward.'

'I ain't no coward.'

'Well, what else would you call a man who finds it necessary to hide behind a woman to save his own neck?'

'Damn you,' said Green, as he pushed Cate, sprawling, onto the deck.

She scrambled to her feet and backed away towards the rail.

Green pushed his knife into his sash and in one swift movement pulled out a flintlock.

Henry heard Cate draw in her breath, as Green aimed his pistol at Henry's chest and pulled the trigger.

Henry heard Cate shout his name before the pistol misfired with a splutter.

He drew his sword.

Green threw the pistol down. 'I'll send yer to a perm'nent grave this time,' he screamed above the sounds of the battle raging around them, and pulled out his cutlass.

Henry sensed a movement behind him and whirled round to see a corsair levelling a pistol at him. Henry whisked his sword, the blade caught the other man neatly in the ribs and without a sound he crumpled to the deck.

'Devil take you!' cried Green, and Henry wheeled back to face the point of Green's gleaming cutlass.

'Oh aye, surely — but not yet,' said

Henry.

Green's lips curled back in a snarl. Over the captain's shoulder, Henry saw one of Green's men fight his way over to seize Cate. She slammed her shoulder into the stocky man, but he caught her.

'Cate!' shouted Henry.

Green lunged forward, thrust his cutlass at Henry's gut and the blades of the two men clashed noisily.

Green struck out at Henry, slashing his cutlass, and each time Henry deflected the pirate's blade. They circled one another, lunging and parrying. Both fought with deadly grimness. The tip of Henry's blade caught Green's shoulder and blood trickled down the front of his shirt. The Violeta's captain staggered back, looked at the blood and roared his anger.

He pressed forward, bellowing obscenities, slashing back and forth like a madman.

Henry felt his sword arm wavering and crimson burst out on his sleeve. He renewed his attack, as his blade hissed and clashed against Green's. Time after time Henry leapt aside, evading Green's deadly thrusts. But the blood from the wound on his arm dripped steadily onto the deck boards and he knew he was losing strength. He prayed that he would not slip on the deck, now slick with the blood of dead and dying men.

Green continued to attack furiously. Tight-lipped with concentration, Henry gradually gained ground, his thrusting blade pushing his opponent back further. Green's breath came uneven and fast, beads of moisture stood out on his forehead.

Suddenly Green lunged at Henry savagely, intent on making an end of it. But with almost his last ounce of strength, Henry blocked the move and the next instant Green's cutlass went flying from the man's grasp. Green lost his footing, tumbled backwards into a bloody puddle and then he was down.

Henry glanced towards Cate in the pirate's firm grasp and saw relief on her white face. The man pushed Cate aside and started forward, his cruel double-edged blade raised. Cate lifted her arm and smashed her elbow into his head. Dazed, the pirate went down onto his knees and struggled to rise.

'No,' said Henry, shaking his head and pointing his sword at Green. 'Another step and I split your captain where he lies.'

'Stay where you are,' said Green bitterly to the other man, who dropped back to his knees.

'Good,' said Henry. 'Put your weapon on the deck and push it towards Miss Trelawny.'

The pirate hesitated, casting an anxious glance at his captain.

Henry shrugged, lowering his point to Green's throat.

'Obey!' screamed Green.

The man laid down his cutlass, his face sullen as he eyed Henry, and slid it across the boards. Cate snatched it up.

'Stay still,' he said to Green. 'Now order the rest of your men to lay down their weapons.'

Green shouted out the order over the noise of the battle. Gradually the hand to hand fighting stopped, as one by one his men reluctantly did as they were instructed. When all the remaining corsairs were silent and subdued, Henry indicated to the men of the Spanish Princess to collect and pile up the weapons.

Ashen-faced, Cate dropped the cutlass onto the pile and ran to Henry. He slipped his unwounded left arm round her shoulder and felt her trembling.

'Thank God you're safe,' she whispered, her voice tearful.

His hair blew about his face and blood oozed from his arm, but for one moment his eyes held hers and they smiled at each other. He pulled her to him, feeling his heart beat loud but steady, keeping his focus on Green.

'Keep these rogues covered with your pistols,' he said to Morgan and three of his crew, once the blades and pistols had been placed in a heap near him. 'And now, Mr Green, you will give your word, under your code of conduct, that you will do nothing if I permit you to rise?'

'Yes, curse you!'

'Pray rise,' said Henry.

He stepped back, rested his sword point on the deck and watched Green climb to his feet.

'What a pity,' snarled Green, 'that our code of conduct doesn't cover this situation.'

Even as the words left Green's mouth, Henry saw him pull a second pistol from his sash and aim it at him. Henry pushed Cate away from him, and suddenly his left shoulder burned with pain where her head had rested just a moment before. He slid to his knees.

Cate landed on the pile of pistols and in a flash she snatched up one, aimed and pulled the trigger. The pistol jerked in her hand and she landed back on the weapons, but Green's snarl died away as a bleeding hole flowered in his chest.

For several long seconds it appeared as though there wasn't a sound on the ship. On Green's face was neither pain or anger — but surprise.

He crumpled to the deck. Cate stood over Green, dazed, staring at his body. 'Let that be a lesson to you all,' said Morgan. 'A woman's fury is a dreadful thing.'

He turned to the crew of the Spanish Princess, who were gazing at Cate in stunned admiration. 'Watch the corsairs,' said Morgan and he gently took the pistol from her unresisting hand. She ran to Henry and dropped to her knees beside him.

'It was him or you,' she said, 'and you are worth twenty of him.' She caught her breath on a sob and he took her hand, wincing at the pain in his shoulder.

She clung to him and he groaned, though he relished feeling her in his arms. 'I rescued you.' He smiled down at her. 'And now you have rescued me.'

Cate brushed the tears from her eyes. Tenderly she helped him to his feet and put her arm around his waist. Side by side they walked, following Morgan as he cleared their way past the subdued prisoners and towards the Spanish Princess, its crew jubilant in victory.

'Mr Morgan,' said Cate. He stopped and turned back. 'Thank you for all you have done these last days, but I must now resume control of my ship. You understand, I hope.'

She straightened her spine and looked every inch the captain again, but Henry standing close could hear her uneven breathing.

'Aye, captain,' Morgan said, with a smile. He stood tall and threw her a naval salute.

She smiled back, then turned again to the deck. The battle was over, but there was work to be done — clearing the debris, swabbing the boards, repairing the damage, seeing to the injured and dead men.

She raised her voice and addressed the Barbary pirates. 'Any of you who wish to join my crew may do so, but you will be closely watched and any misdemeanours punished severely.'

She turned back to Morgan. 'Put the rest in a boat and cast them adrift. They will be picked up by other pirates, I dare say.

'Do what you can for the injured. Gather up the captured weapons and distribute them among our men. Make the Violeta fast, arrange for the corsairs to take turns rowing her, get the carpenter to repair the stern as best he can, and keep some of our men on board and have them sail her behind us.'

'Aye, Captain,' said Morgan. 'Oh, and ma'am ... ?'

'Yes, Mr Morgan?'

'We're all pleased to have you back.' He grinned broadly.

She laughed. 'As I am pleased to be back, believe me!'

As Henry and Cate returned to the Spanish Princess, a cheer broke out from her crew on board. Henry saw the relief on their faces and the obvious respect they had for Cate. He nodded his gratitude at the men and, in a voice that sounded faint to his own ears, added his thanks for their part in the rescue mission.

'Now you must rest in my cabin. You

are bleeding heavily.' Her voice came soft in his ear. 'You have been hurt for my sake. You must now lean on me.' She slid herself under his shoulder.

With a great effort Henry controlled the inclination to pass out, and he lifted her hand to his lips.

'My heart was in my mouth when we fired on the corsairs' ship,' he said quietly. 'However, I knew if we didn't fire, they would have us, but I aimed merely to disable her, nothing more. I knew I had to have you back, because you are part of my heart.'

'Hush,' she said, but her eyes shone with love. 'Save your strength.'

When they reached her cabin, Morgan following close behind, Henry reeled and would have fallen, had Cate's hands not caught and steadied him. She cast an anxious glance at Morgan.

Henry managed a faint smile. 'It's nothing.'

'Carry him to my couch, Mr Morgan. Oh, do take care with his poor shoulder.'

Taking Henry's weight, Morgan helped

him across the cabin. Henry gasped as a pain shot through his shoulder when he was lowered onto the bed, then his feet were lifted to lie on top of her blanket. With a sigh, he felt Cate settle him gently against the cushions.

He saw Morgan whisper in Cate's ear and she turned a little pale, but she spoke briskly. 'I do not think it wise to move Mr Darley again, so I will need your cabin for myself, Mr Morgan. Please send one of the men to me with hot water. I will tend to Mr Darley's wounds.'

'Aye, Captain.'

She began to ease off Henry's blood-stained shirt and he gritted his teeth to stop a groan escaping his lips.

'Just a moment,' she said, anguish in her voice. She ran to her cupboard and pulled out a pair of scissors. 'This will be less painful.'

'You are going to stab my heart?' he said, with a feeble attempt at humour.

Cate smiled. 'I prefer your heart intact.' She cut off his shirt and tenderly removed it, and threw it aside.

'The slash on your arm is not serious,' she said carefully. 'As to your shoulder, the bullet has passed through. It went high, just catching your flesh, and I think there can be no damage to the bone, but I do not like the look of the wound.'

Henry made no attempt at a response; his thoughts were becoming harder to gather and the cabin would not stay in focus. He closed his eyes and as if from a distance heard a door open, a metal bowl being set down on the wooden floor, and Cate thanking someone before the door closed again.

He felt her gently sponge his shoulder with warm water, and heard her murmur, 'If only this bleeding would stop.'

He opened his eyes and saw Cate studying his face. He wanted to gather her in his arms, but his body would not oblige.

'Thank you for what you have done for me,' she said softly.

Dream-like, Henry watched her bind up his wounds as tightly as she could, and go to a cupboard to measure out a cordial, which she obliged him to swallow.

'It will ease your pain.'

He remembered her settling him comfortably, placing her cool hand on his hot brow, and seating herself next to him on the couch, taking his hand.

'Now you must rest,' she said.

He could barely keep his eyes open, but he was aware of her gown with its hem torn off, her bare ankles above feet shod in silk slippers, and he murmured, 'You look pretty in that dress,' before he surrendered to the draw of sleep.

12

Sick at heart for the terrible waste of her men who had fallen, Cate went about her tasks. Three of her men had serious wounds and four were dead. One of the dead was the doctor, and it was this news that Morgan had whispered to her when he placed Henry on the couch.

Repairs to the Spanish Princess could be done at sea. It was a quieted crew that now worked. As she sat by Henry's sick bed, Cate heard only hammers and saws.

She was desperately worried about Henry. The fever of infection had appeared in him. She tenderly brushed back a lock of hair from his burning forehead. *All this has happened because of me*, she thought. *I was too quick to jump to conclusions.*

Henry tossed and turned, muttering incoherently. She gently sponged his face with lavender water and it seemed to soothe him. But when she rose to move away from the bed, his hand grasped her wrist.

'Don't leave me,' he muttered.

Throughout the next three days she bathed his forehead, persuaded him to sip water and kept him as comfortable as possible. With young Robert's help, she changed his bandages, careful not to hurt the ugly wound.

'That is much better,' Henry said with a sigh of content. 'You have such a light touch, Cate.'

'That is because you are such a good patient.' She smiled to keep the concern from her face.

The days passed. They sailed through the Strait of Gibraltar with its great rock and dolphins playing at their bows. Cate pored over navigation charts with as much attention as she could muster. Gradually the crew's high spirits returned.

Henry came slowly back to life. He opened his eyes wearily, turned his head to where she sat by his bed and his eyes widened in faint surprise.

'Thank God!' she said. 'The fever has broken.' She laid a gentle hand on his brow and smiled down into his eyes. She felt a renewed surge of tenderness at the painful leanness of his bearded face and the deadly pallor beneath the tanned skin.

He returned the smile weakly. 'I just need to sleep.' His lids drooped shut and he drifted into a peaceful slumber.

★ ★ ★

The following morning, Cate was at her desk writing in the ship's log when she heard Henry stir. She glanced up and saw him blink in the sunlight streaming through the open porthole.

She laid down the quill and went to him. His warm smile reminded her of the day they met on the hill in Azul. That seemed so long ago now.

He raised himself on his elbow, grimacing at the pain the movement caused him. 'Have I been here long?'

She eased him back onto the cushions. 'Be still. You must not aggravate the wound. You have been here almost a seven-night.'

'So long?'

'Yes. And what a fright you gave me.'

She smiled to make light of her comment, but she did not miss the deep furrow of pain between his brows. 'I have not been able to thank you properly for what you did. Green would have killed me.'

'You were not harmed then, Cate?'

'You need have no fear.'

He reached for her hand and his warm fingers closed around hers. 'I owe you my life.'

She smiled. 'Then we are equal.'

She bent over him, gently arranging the pillows to support his shoulder.

'You are strong, Henry. You will make a full recovery.' Her fingers lightly touched the blonde shadows on his cheek. 'I will send one of my men to shave you.'

He covered her hand with his against his cheek.

'You need nourishment,' she said with a smile, sliding her hand out. 'I will go and get some broth for you.'

Later, she washed herself and slipped into clean clothes. Before sailing from Azul, Morgan had bundled up her belongings from the Ancle Posada. *Dear Abella*, she thought, *once we are back in Cornwall I will get a message to you.*

Cate stood in front of the small, cracked glass in Morgan's cabin and pinned up her damp hair. She remembered standing in front of her own tall looking-glass on the day she encountered pirate captain Lovett and she smiled. How much had happened since then.

★ ★ ★

Henry recovered quickly, each day making great progress. Hardly a fortnight later, he was up and dressed and quite himself again, his shoulder only a little tender.

He had just tied back his newly-washed hair when there came a knock on the cabin door. He called for the person to enter.

'You look much improved,' said Cate,

entering.

'Come, sit on the divan next to me and we can talk,' he said.

She did as he bid. 'Are you quite comfortable?'

Henry smiled. 'Yes, I thank you, señorita.'

'We have so much to say that it is difficult to know where to start.' She hesitated, then the words tumbled out. 'I thought you had drowned!'

Her voice caught at his heart. 'And I believed the same of you.'

'Henry, what happened on that terrible night we were shipwrecked?'

'I will answer as best I can,' he said, soberly. 'I was washed up on the rocky part of the island. Elphick and I were the only ones left alive there.'

'Elphick!' Cate started. 'Where is he now?'

'He did not survive his wounds,' said Henry.

'Oh!'

'When I could not find you, I thought at first that the sea had claimed you,' he said quietly. 'Cate, I'm sorry for not believing you when you said the light could be wreckers.'

'Do not think of that,' she said. 'We both knew we had no choice but to seek land.'

He drew in a deep breath and told her of his days on the island, the appearance of the Spanish Princess, their pursuit of the corsairs.

Cate shuddered. 'Thank God you didn't give me up for dead.'

'I could not have done that.' He pressed her hand. 'I can only imagine what terrors you must have been through.'

She looked down at their joined hands. 'Now it is your turn to ask questions.'

'I have only one.' He paused, flushing with self-consciousness and anger. 'Tell me what happened with Green.'

'There is little to tell of him. When I woke on the island it must have been about mid-day.'

'Mid-day?' said Henry. 'Why, at that moment I was lying unconscious at the other end of the island. If only — '

'You could not have known,' said Cate, stilling him. 'Green took me onto his ship. We were making for the slave market when you appeared.'

'How did Green treat you?'

Her fingers tightened in his. 'He tried to ravish me,' she said simply. 'But I reminded him that an unharmed female would bring him a better price.'

'The devil!' cried Henry. 'He deserved to die.'

'Tell me about Elphick. He died of his injuries?'

Henry let go of her hand and met her eyes. 'I should confess to you that the injuries were from my sword ... '

Cate frowned. 'What do you mean?'

'He told me about your father's last voyage.'

She stared at him. 'What could Elphick know about that?'

'I'm afraid it will be distressing for you to hear the details.'

'Just tell me plainly what he said.'

'Very well.' Henry's voice was gentle. 'It was he who fatally wounded your father.'

She paled and sank back against the cushions. 'Elphick,' she said quietly.

As Henry recounted what Elphick had told him, the look of shock grew on Cate's face.

'Yes,' she said, 'my father did have a ship's boy called Jacob. I never knew his family name nor Jacob himself. The battle in which he was killed took place before I began accompanying my father on his journeys.'

'Privateering is a dangerous life,' said Henry. 'John Trelawny was not to blame for the lad's death, but that made no difference to Elphick.'

'He would have been grief-stricken to lose his child, I can see that,' said Cate.

'There is worse to come, I'm afraid. After the death of their son, Elphick's wife fell into a deep melancholy and took her own life.'

'Dear God.' Cate hung her head. A thought struck her. 'I thought the name Elphick was familiar when he introduced himself to me, but he said we had never met. That anyway was true.' She rose and looked out of the porthole. 'That explains his hatred of my father.'

'And, I'm afraid,' said Henry quietly, 'his hatred of you.'

She spun round. 'What do you mean?'

'Elphick tried to kill you on Azul. He admitted it to me.'

'On the cliff-top, the harbour ... ' She sank back down onto the divan. 'Elphick wasn't successful with me — but he was with my father.'

'He didn't set out to kill your father. By pure chance he was on the French vessel when its path crossed that of John Trelawny. He recognised the Spanish Princess and acted on the spur of the moment.' Henry took her hands once more. 'After that, he knew what he wanted. The death of Trelawny's daughter.'

'This is almost too much to take in,' she said, her voice faltering. 'How did Elphick come to be on the Oceanus?'

'It is something I very much regret. When he heard that my chief mate was to retire and I was in need of a new man, he presented himself for the position. He hoped your ship and mine would meet, and I believe he felt there was justice in taking revenge where it had all started — on the high seas,' said Henry gently.

She lowered her gaze, not meeting his eyes, and he saw a flush cross her cheeks.

His heart tightened. He had fallen in love, he could not deny it. But what future could they have together? He was a pirate, acting outside the law. The threat of capture, trial and death was something he had accepted since taking on this life — but it was different for Cate.

Her dark eyes were searching his face. 'Cate,' he said, 'I care for you, but I am a pirate, a common felon.'

'None of us is perfect,' she said, and there was a smile in her eyes.

He laughed to hide his anguish. 'Well, soon we will be back in England.'

'And we can resume our normal lives.'

'Is that what you would wish?'

'Perhaps,' she said in a tight voice.

Somewhere above them on deck two men were singing a shanty as they worked. The sun shone through the porthole, bathing the cabin in gold. But for Henry the world was suddenly a dark, uncertain place.

His voice deepened. 'Thank you for all your kindnesses during my illness, but now that my health returns, I will relinquish your cabin to you and sleep below deck with the rest of the crew until we reach England.'

He kissed the tips of her fingers, rose and strode out of the cabin, his heart heavy. Somehow, he had to make everything right.

13

As night fell, Cate remained for a long while at her table, looking at but not seeing navigation charts. She rubbed a hand across her forehead. She pushed back her chair and crossed the cabin to stare out of the porthole. 'What happened?' she asked the empty sea.

I shall never know love, she thought, hating her inability to declare her love, for she could not be certain that Henry felt the same way towards her.

She could hardly bear to look at him — his beautifully carved mouth, the aristocratic nose, the firm chin — lest the temptation to throw herself into his arms should prove too great.

When at last, listless and tired, she was about to withdraw to bed, a man's voice lifted in song from the deck above. She listened, not recognising the voice. It stirred her heart. The man was singing an old ballad in the ancient Celtic language of Cornwall. It told of a young girl waiting for her sailor love to return from sea ...

I scan the ocean, a sail to see. Will it ever come, my love, to comfort me?

Never had she heard anyone sing like this. His velvety voice rose and fell, like the waves of the ocean. She caught her reflection in the tall looking-glass, her eyes open wide.

How foolish I am! She laughed to herself. *What do I care?* But she opened the door, crept up the steps and emerged onto the deck.

He sat on a coil of rope and as Cate approached he stopped singing and hummed softly. The night was cloudy and it was too dark for her to see his expression as she settled herself by his feet, but she knew it was Henry. 'Sing again,' she pleaded, all at once shy.

His warm voice rose once more, softer now. She closed her eyes. His voice filled her with a delight she had never experienced before and she felt giddy with pleasure.

261

He fell silent. He leaned towards her and his hand lifted her chin with gentleness. Her eyes fastened upon his shadowy lips and she watched, trembling a little, as his head descend slowly towards her own. As soon as his mouth touched hers, her head swam. Oh, she did not know that a man's lips could be so soft! With closed eyes she abandoned herself to the kiss as waves of pleasure surged through her.

Confused at such feelings, she shuddered and pulled back, rose and went to stand against the deck rail. She heard Henry's footsteps behind her and he turned her gently towards him.

'Did you not enjoy that?' he asked, in a throaty voice that made her heart thud.

She wanted to laugh and cry at the same time, but she didn't know why.

'I hope you did,' he said, a slow smile curling his lips, 'for I intend to do it again.'

His arm encircled her waist and he lowered his lips to hers. Now she listened to her emotions and she kissed him back, burning in his embrace.

When he pulled away, it was to rest his forehead against hers. His breath came as quickly as did hers. 'There is nothing in the world I want as much as I want you.'

'Is it possible that we can share a future?'

'I hope so,' he said, drawing back to look into her eyes. But then he grinned, turned her around and slapped her rump. 'But for now, we should each get some sleep.'

Laughter bubbled out of her before she could stop herself. But she turned back and saw he looked very satisfied. She gathered up her skirts, ran across the deck and down the steps. When she reached her cabin she was still laughing.

She undressed in haste and jumped into bed. The face of the man she had once hated rose before her eyes, but now she burned at the memory of the pleasure she had felt in his arms.

* * *

The next few days flew by. Cate had resumed the role of captain. Henry asked to be allowed to take a share of the ship's work as his strength fully returned.

Cate accepted at last that she was very much in love with Henry.

It seemed to her, as they sat side by side at the desk, working on charts and calculations, or talking of other ships and far-off countries, that she had never known happiness before. With their shoulders touching, his hands beside hers, she was filled with a glow and a shameless longing to be closer still.

She looked away from him, out through the porthole and across the sea, fearful that he might read the message in her eyes. It was almost too much to believe that he might really love her.

The morning brought a cheerful sight through the portholes of her cabin. The sun had risen and slowly the wind stirred and the large sail swelled. Cate came up on deck to take the morning air and revelled in the ship racing through the fresh sea. She heard her crew laugh and sing, happy to be on their way home. Now and again the spray broke on the deck and the wind played with her hair. Her heart swelled until she felt it might take over her entire being.

By noon she was hungry and there came the smell of hot coffee. Presently Henry climbed to the deck, carrying a tray. She took it from him and they sat side by side, leaning against the bulwark, savouring cheese with the hard biscuit. She poured steaming coffee from the jug into two cups and they drank, watching each other over the rims.

He smiled but said nothing.

She laughed, putting down her cup and lifting her arms to arrange her disordered locks. Henry pulled from his pocket a slim chain and held it on his upturned palm, the gold links dangling through his fingers.

'My lost chain!' she cried.

'I found it on the beach,' he told her. 'Turn around.'

She did so, holding her curls in one hand high on the back of her head.

He drew the chain around her neck. Shielded from the eyes of her crew by the bulwark, his lips brushed the nape of her neck and her heart leapt.

She turned back and smiled, and he said, 'May I give the men an order?'

'What sort of an order?' she asked, surprised. 'We are almost home.'

'You will see, if you will allow me to do so?'

She knew now that she trusted him completely and she nodded. Henry called out the order to make for the land ahead of them to the west. They gazed as little by little the line of the coast became distinct.

'Do you know where we are going?' he asked.

'I can see we are making for Penzance.'

'Almost,' he said. 'Lamorna.' He smiled, watching her as he did so, until at last she looked away, self-conscious under his scrutiny.

She stared out over the smooth sea towards the land and the smell of it came to her with the breeze. Warm cliff grass and hot sand where the sun had shone all day. She knew that, whatever had occurred in the past, at this moment she was content.

A smile lifting her lips, she glanced up at him. 'What is in Lamorna that makes us bound there?'

'We are to visit the special cargo for which your father gave his life,' he said.

★ ★ ★

A few houses perched precariously on the hillside. The colours shimmered and shifted, the air trembled in the heat, flowers bloomed on the rough grass. The Spanish Princess dropped anchor on the fringe of a little bay with a stretch of white sand.

For a moment or so the colony of gulls, nesting on the cliffs above, became restive. Their uneasy cries echoed against the cliff face and travelled across the water. They settled again and the silence was unbroken.

Cate stood against the rail of the deck.

Henry stood beside her and she saw him trying to read the mixture of emotions in her face.

'I don't understand,' she said. 'Morgan and the crew said there had been no cargo.'

'But that isn't quite what happened. All will become clear very soon, I promise.'

Her life had been turned upside down when her father was killed and Cate was afraid that it would turn again now, just when she was almost unbearably happy.

There was silence between them for a moment. *I must lay to rest the events of that day*, she thought to herself.

'We will use the small boat. There is insufficient wind to take us into the cove. Besides,' he said, 'I wish to row you there myself.'

A ladder had been thrown over the ship's side and a boat waited below. Henry climbed down and held the tiller. Cate followed and took the tiller from him as he bent to the oars. He rowed strongly over the water, his face betraying no pain from the shoulder wound, his shirt sleeves pushed up, powerful muscles standing out in his forearms. When the bow touched the sand, Henry bounded out and pulled the boat from the wash.

The skirts of the cliffs thrust out into the sea in two ridges, forming an inlet. He turned, smiled encouragement and took her hand. There was no sound but the wash of the waves breaking upon the shore and the crunch of their feet as they crossed onto the shingle.

They rounded the coastline and she saw a small cottage set back from the beach. From its doorway a trim, elderly man stepped forward.

'Señor Garcia?' said Henry.

The man nodded and took Henry's outstretched hand. 'I saw your sloop from my window,' he said, 'pulling what looks like a pirates' galley.'

'The spoils of war,' said Henry.

Garcia lifted Cate's hand and kissed it. 'Please, come this way.'

Still bewildered, Cate let herself be ushered into a sitting-room with a small arched window facing the sea.

'Please, take a seat. You must drink some wine with me.' He poured from the decanter on a table at the side of the room and handed one glass to Cate, another to Henry and lifted his own. 'To John Trelawny, God rest his soul.'

'John Trelawny,' echoed Henry.

'I imagine he is the reason you are here,' said Garcia.

'You knew my father?' said Cate, at last finding her tongue.

'Ah, you are Señor Trelawny's daughter?' He peered at her. 'I am sorry I was not able to make your father's acquaintance, but be assured he was a brave man.'

'Thank you,' said Cate.

'Señor,' said Henry, 'I am Henry Darley. Forgive us for arriving unannounced. We are here because Miss Trelawny wishes to learn about the special cargo carried that day by the Spanish Princess.'

'The special cargo . . . ' said Señor Garcia, with a small smile. 'Was that the term they used? I remember the day clearly.' A shadow crossed his face. 'I was on the

French ship.'

'You were on the enemy ship?' Cate put down her glass and felt her cheeks burn red.

'Not willingly.' He stared out of the window. 'The ship was sailing from Spain, where I had been captured by the French, and it was making for France. I realised something was amiss when I heard the call to battle. The French ship let loose a hail of bullets onto a sloop at the mouth of a small bay.'

'What happened next?' asked Cate, unable to take her eyes from him.

He turned back into the room. 'In the chaos of the fighting, my cabin door was left unguarded and I slipped out. When the French launched their boarding party, I managed to escape onto the Spanish Princess.'

Cate could see Garcia was reliving the moment in his memory.

'The deck of the English ship was swarming with Frenchmen. I took a sword from a fallen man and fought for the English. Above the shouting and

fighting, I heard the captain give
order to get the Spanish Princess
of the bay. Your father fought like a
n, Miss Trelawny, but before the sloop
arted to come about a man stepped out
from behind a barrel.'

Señor Garcia paused, and when he
spoke again his voice was full of pity.

'I saw the Englishman from the French
ship single out John Trelawny and plunge
his sword into him. I have thought about
this killer many times since. He did not
join the battle, he waited to attack only
your father.' He turned his sympathetic
gaze onto Cate.

She fought back tears. Henry rose
from his seat and came to stand behind
her. He placed a gentle hand on her
shoulder.

'The men of the Spanish Princess
fought on,' said Garcia. 'Some of the
crew were able to loose her sail and she
ploughed back onto the open sea.'

'I am truly sorry for what happened to
you, señor,' said Cate, her face pale. 'But
I don't understand what it has to do with

the command my father received.'

'Because the special cargo on the ship John Trelawny came to collect was me.'

Cate stared at him. 'Forgive me,' she said, 'but who are you?'

'Shall we go into the garden?' said Garcia. 'The fresh air might do you good.'

She nodded and rose, her thoughts in turmoil. Henry tucked her hand into his arm and they followed Señor Garcia out of the cottage, and onto a path bordered by sea pinks rippling in the breeze.

'That's better,' murmured Henry, bending his head to hers. 'The colour is coming back into your cheeks.'

Garcia stopped by a wooden bench with a view out to sea. 'From here we can admire the Spanish Princess.'

Her sloop lay at anchor in the late afternoon sun and Cate experienced a sudden warmth of pride in her ship — and in her father. He had gone to rescue the captured Spaniard and, although he had not known it, he had been success-ful.

Henry sat by her side and she was grateful for his solid presence.

Garcia lowered himself onto the bench at her other side. 'I was a courtier at the Spanish Royal Court. There I was privy to a number of secrets. Such a person will always be welcome to a foreign king. It is rumoured that my country's king is impotent and the Habsburg line will die with him. He is known as El Hechizado, the Hexed. When King Charles dies there will undoubtedly be civil war in Spain.' He sighed. 'The Austrian Habsburgs consider themselves the rightful heirs of Charles. The French monarchy wish to take over the Spanish Crown. The Spanish and Austrian branches of the House of Habsburg, and the Bourbon monarchs of France and Spain, will wage war against one another.'

Henry had remained respectfully quiet throughout Garcia's account, but now he spoke. 'A trusted and loyal privateer was needed to intercept the French ship and bring Señor Garcia to Britain. That man was your father, Cate.'

'I don't know what to think any more.' She turned back to Garcia. 'What happened once you were on my father's ship, señor?'

He looked down at his hands, folded in his lap. 'I fought against the Frenchmen for as long as I dare. But, not wishing to be captured again by them, I crept into the hold on the Spanish Princess and hid there. Once we were sailing, I stole food from the kitchen when I was able. I did not know then that the attack had been a rescue mission by the British Crown to free me! The captain was seriously injured, so I could not throw myself on his mercy, and I was apprehensive as to what the crew might do if I revealed myself. Thankfully, the wind picked up and the voyage was short.'

'What did you do when the ship dropped anchor in Cornwall? You must have known no one there.'

He nodded. 'I waited until dark, then I slipped away. Once on shore, I knew only that I had to get to London, to the Royal Court, where I was sure I would be welcome. But until then I was at the mercy of all and sundry, having no money and no friends to help me. I scavenged in gutters in towns and begged for food from farmhouses, I slept in streets and fields. Sometimes a driver would let me travel in his cart, at other times I walked. After eighteen long days I reached London. I was dirty, dishevelled, hungry and tired. My accent and what I had to tell persuaded a courtier that I should be hastened in for an audience with the King. His Majesty was happy to see me, as he'd feared the rescue mission had failed.'

Cate knew that if it had not been for Garcia, her father would still be alive. But he had done what was right.

'When the King asked me why Captain Trelawny had not brought me to the Palace, I told him I had never met this captain and had escaped on a trading ship the French had attacked. He protested that he'd sent the Spanish Princess to rescue me. Then I remembered seeing her name as I slipped off the ship. It is not as if I could mistake a name like that.'

Henry took her hand, and she drew strength from his touch. She said, 'I am glad my father did not die in vain.'

'Indeed he did not, my dear,' said Garcia. 'I owe my life to John Trelawny. Without him, I would now be a prisoner — or worse — in France.'

He bent forward, plucked a pink flower from the side of the path and presented it to Cate. 'But now it is my turn to ask a question. How did you know I was living here?'

Cate looked to Henry for the answer.

'It was Elphick who informed me just before he died,' said Henry.

'Elphick!' Cate could not keep the surprise from her voice. Always this man!

'I could make out very little of what he said, he was so weak,' Henry said, turning to her, 'but I heard 'Garcia', a name which meant nothing to me, and 'Lamorna', which I knew was along this coastline.'

'But how did Elphick know?'

'He'd overheard gossip at an inn, a rumour about the whereabouts of a missing Spaniard.'

'Perhaps, in telling you, Elphick was trying to make amends. I hope I can forgive him one day.' Cate touched the sea pink with a finger. 'There is one final question I must ask. The man who killed my father — can you describe him to me?'

'He was tall and thin, and wore a black coat.'

'Oh!' She glanced at Henry, whose face betrayed nothing. 'Did this man also wear a black hat with a long red feather?' she asked.

'No.' Garcia drew his brows together. 'He wore a blue cap, and a kerchief over the lower part of his face. And he held his sword in his left hand, which is unusual.'

'Left hand?' Cate searched her memory for a half-remembered image. A man smoothing his hair with the palm of his left hand by the harbour, fondling the crucifix on the breast of the young serving girl at Abella's inn, reaching for Cate on the cliff top …

'Elphick was left-handed.' She glanced up at Henry. 'Oh, I accused you of murder and then, worse, tried to kill you! It is unforgiveable.'

'I expect I will eventually forgive you,' said Henry, a teasing gleam in his eyes.

★ ★ ★

When Cate and Henry left Señor Garcia, the sun was low over the sea. They made their way along the shingles down to the beach and there Cate turned to face Henry.

'I am truly sorry for being too quick to judge you,' said Cate. 'But there is still one thing I need to understand. When my fathered whispered 'Lovett' as he lay dying, what did he mean?'

Henry shook his head. 'I don't know.'

'Oh dear, what a mess I have made.'

'Not it all,' said Henry, 'for otherwise we might never have met.'

She glanced up at him from under her

lashes. 'Perhaps we don't have to return to the Spanish Princess just yet . . . '

He laughed softly. 'Let us sit here for a while.'

He handed her down onto the sand and lowered himself next to her. Removing the sea pink she still held, with gentle fingers he slipped it behind her ear. With a contented sigh, she turned her face to the setting sun. The only sound was the sigh of waves and the call of a gull before it settled for the night.

After a long moment, Henry said, 'You are a remarkable young woman, Cate. Brave and passionate. When you believe in something, you are determined.'

'To the point of obstinacy!'

His lips twitched. 'But who is to say what is obstinacy and what is determination?'

'I have been worse than foolish. I don't know how you have managed to put up with me.' His gaze was on her face and he was so close.

'I have not had much choice,' he said with a wicked grin, 'for we have been in

280

close quarters on one ship or another for much of our acquaintance.'

If she looked at him now, he would see the love in her eyes. Could she do this, reveal herself completely in this way? When she looked up into his blue eyes, she read his answering love.

He took her face in his hands and kissed her. His arms pulled her close and she burned in his embrace. Through his shirt she could feel his heart pounding and she trembled.

'At last, my love … You have either scowled at me, or tried to attack me, or — '

'Enough!' She laid a finger on his lips. 'I will change. I have changed.'

He took her hand, turned it over and kissed the inside of her wrist. 'But I want you just the way you are.'

She blushed deeply —— she, the brave captain of a privateer ship. He laughed deep in his throat and kissed her again and again, until she believed beyond doubt that he loved her.

14

Cate stood on the prow of the Spanish Princess as the ship plunged through the blue-grey sea, bound for Falmouth, the Violeta in her wake. The white sails stretched and sang above her head. All the sounds that she loved came to her ears: the straining of ropes, the thud of wind in the rigging, and the voices of her men laughing with one another. The sun shone upon her bare head and when the spray blew back upon the deck the taste came to her lips.

This day, she thought, is a day to be held and cherished forever. *I love Henry, and he loves me, and nothing else matters.*

She looked to where he sat with his back against the bulwark, eyes closed and hands behind his head. He opened his eyes and looked at her, rose and stretched. He came and stood behind her at the rail. They stood watching the sky, the sea and the sails, with no need to speak.

The coast of Falmouth was on the horizon and gulls came to greet them, wheeling and crying above the masts. Leaning against him, she watched the harbour growing more distinct as the rumble of the town drift out to them.

The breeze freshened.

'Cold, my love?' said Henry.

'Never.' As Henry's arms slid around her shoulders. She thought every day now is a gift.

★   ★   ★

The sun went down, a depth came to the trees and the still-warm fragrance of day hovered in the air. With the Spanish Princess and her prize, the Violeta, moored at Falmouth, Henry rowed the small boat, water lapping at its sides, towards the cove at Pentreath Castle. Cate looked up and watched the first star.

Soon a fire glowed on the shingle beach, the dry sticks cracking, and while

Henry toasted bread and cooked bacon, she brewed coffee in the old pot he had brought from that beach, so long ago now it seemed.

When they had eaten their fill, he settled against a rock and she leaned against his knee.

'This,' she said, watching the flames, 'could be our life forever if we wished. In other countries, on other seas.'

'Yes,' he said, 'if we so wished. But is this what you really want? You may wish for another life one day soon, with a household and babies.'

'A ship can also be a household and children reared on it.'

He smiled. 'Children need somewhere safe, a permanent home.'

He is right, she thought, the breath catching in her throat. She looked up at him, but he was no longer smiling. He bent towards the fire, as if seeking its warmth, and the flames illuminated his face and throat.

'Do you remember the day we first met?' he said. 'Were you angry with me for attacking the Spanish Princess?'

'No,' she said, 'only ashamed that I did not stop to plunder your ship!'

'And that decision shows,' he said, turning back to her, 'You will never make a pirate.' She forced herself to ask, 'What will you do now?' He waited a moment, his eyes unreadable in the light of the fire. 'I suppose I must set sail again,' he said, stroking her curls, 'for I am an outlaw.'

She took his hand and pressed it against her cheek.

'When morning comes,' he went on carefully, 'there will be the realisation that a life together is impossible.'

She shivered. 'That sounds like a farewell.'

'My love, it is.'

'I don't understand. Why must you go?'

'With my history, I cannot be a proper husband for you.'

'This is nonsense,' she said, alarm in her voice. 'Whatever dangers are to be faced, I will face them with you. I can only be fully alive if I am with you.'

He looked over her head, towards the dark sea. 'It's the way of the world,' he said. 'You are Catherina Trelawny, acting under authority from the King, and I am a pirate and an enemy to all.'

She looked up at him. 'You could cease to be a pirate.'

'It would not signify. Because of my past deeds, there is a price on my head. You know the penalty for being a pirate is execution.'

'I want to be with you,' she repeated.

A tiny breeze stirred her curls and his eyes glittered in the light of the dying embers. He turned his head away and his voice was thick with emotion. 'I cannot allow you to make that sacrifice.'

'I would not call it a sacrifice!' she said, her voice growing stronger.

'It would make no difference what you call it, it would ruin your life and that must never be.'

'But I love you and I am under no illusions.'

There was a long silence, then Henry murmured, 'You deserve better. I pray that you will, in time, forget me.'

She sat still, while above them the stars blazed like gems in the night sky.

'I see,' she whispered at last.

He took her fingers and kissed them. He rose to help her to her feet.

'I return tonight to Falmouth,' he said, 'and your men will bring the Spanish Princess to Pentreath tomorrow. New crew for the Violeta will be recruited and when repairs are made we will leave with the next tide.'

'Henry,' she said, desperate to keep him, 'Look me in the eye and tell me that you do not love me. If you can do that, then I will never think of you again.'

He raised his head and a flush mantled his cheekbones. 'I cannot,' he whispered.

But he seemed to hesitate.

'What is it?' she said. 'Have you have thought of something?'

'There may be a chance ... just a chance ... that if I went to the King and pleaded the error of my ways, he would grant me a Pardon.'

'I will come with you!'

He took her hand. 'It would not be safe. His Majesty is as likely to have me arrested as pardoned. If that happened, you would be taken too, as my accomplice.'

She lifted her chin. 'I will take that chance.'

Henry looked down at her, as tears formed in her eyes. 'Very well.'

Whatever happened, they would not be parted.

'I will tell Morgan and pack a bag. Do not go without me!'

With a laugh that sounded almost wild to her ears, she picked up her skirts and ran up the grassy slope, her heels flying, and burst into the great hall.

'Mr Morgan,' she said breathlessly, pausing for the briefest of moments. 'I am going to St James's Palace with Henry, to petition the King for a Pardon.'

Morgan stood bemused in the middle of the hall. 'And is your maid going, too, my lady?'

'There is no time for that,' she called,

bounding up the wide staircase, the candles in their sconces flickering as she passed.

From the cupboard in her chamber, Cate pulled out a good dress, snatched up other items and threw everything into a leather bag.

Morgan was still in the great hall when Cate ran back down the stairs. She came to a halt in front of him.

'Goodbye, Mr Morgan,' she said, pressing his hand and releasing it. 'Thank you for everything.'

'Are you sure this is the right thing to do, madam?' His eyes crinkled with concern.

'Yes,' she said, her voice firm.

He nodded. 'Then don't keep his lordship waiting.' As Cate stepped out into the darkness, she was sure she heard Morgan call softly, 'Good luck, Cate, my dear.'

Henry was waiting for her on the beach.

They rowed in silence, and she heard only the soft splash of the oars and the beating of her own heart.

In Falmouth, as if in a dream, Cate let herself be led onto a ship sailing for London.

She slept, and when she opened her eyes in the half-light of early morning, the sky was hard and white, and the sea lay like a sheet of silver. The gulls started up their plaintive cry.

She washed and dressed in her pale blue gown, and went onto the deck.

Henry was there. He smiled, pulled her to him and she tasted the salt on his lips.

'Are you happy?' he asked, drawing back to look at her.

'Yes.' She returned his smile, and tried not to think of what might happen when they reached the Palace and had to face the King.

★ ★ ★

At St James's, Cate was by his side when Henry presented himself as the Earl of Lovett and requested an audience with His Majesty.

290

They were left to kick their heels in the antechamber, before a footman returned.

'His Majesty will see you,' said the servant. 'And the lady.'

'It is not necessary that Miss Trelawny attends,' said Henry quickly, casting a concerned look at her.

'Nevertheless,' said the footman, 'His Majesty wishes to see her too.'

'Of course,' said Cate, not meeting Henry's eye. 'It will be an honour.'

They followed the servant down long passages and through splendidly-decorated rooms, until the man signalled for them to wait at a large, heavy door. He turned the brass handle and beckoned for them to follow.

'Your Majesty. Henry Darley, Earl of Lovett, and Miss Catherina Trelawny.'

The King sat on a large, ornate chair resting on a dais at the end of the opulent room. Cate felt Henry squeeze her hand, but she did not take her eyes from the figure of the King with his long, dark wig, pale, slender face, and orange frock coat under an ermine cloak. Cate took a deep breath and followed Henry along the red carpet.

'Your Majesty.' Henry gave a respectful bow.

Cate lowered her eyes and dipped a curtsy. As she came up slowly, she raised her eyes and saw the King was smiling at her.

'Trelawny?' said His Majesty. 'Captain of the Spanish Princess? Why, that's the very ship I sent to rescue Garcia.'

Cate smiled. 'Yes, Your Majesty. John Trelawny was my father.'

The King gave a solemn nod. 'Indeed, I was most sad to learn of his death. A brave and honourable man.'

'Thank you, sire.'

He turned to Henry. 'What is it you wish?'

'Sire,' said Henry, 'Four years ago Your Majesty graciously offered a Pardon to all pirates who surrendered.' The King gave a slow nod, his direct gaze on Henry. Henry continued, his voice steady. 'The Proclamation stated that any pirate who refused to surrender within a twelve-month would be pursued and destroyed, and they would never again be granted mercy.'

Cate bit back an exclamation as an image flew into her mind of Henry being paraded across London Bridge, his body left hanging at Execution Dock for the tides to wash over his head.

'Your Majesty,' said Henry, dipping his head, 'I deeply regret that for some years I have lived the life of a pirate.'

Cate saw the King stiffen and his fingers clutch the gilt arms of his chair.

'Yes?' His low voice carried a warning.

'And I wish to beg your forgiveness, sire,' said Henry soberly. 'I want nothing more than to return to an honest life as the Earl of Lovett and one of your most loyal subjects.'

The King stared at him for some moments as Cate's heart thudded. Then he said, 'You did not ask for a Pardon when we offered them, so pray tell me what has brought about this sudden change of heart?'

'I had not then met Miss Trelawny,' he said. 'She is the only treasure I now desire.'

Cate drew in her breath and watched the King. He was frowning at Henry. *No*, she thought, *it is over*. She fought back a sob.

Then the King suddenly winked! 'Well said, sir. How true it is that the tender emotion can reform a wicked man.' He gave Henry a rakish grin.

Henry drew Cate towards him. 'I wish to marry this lady.'

'Do not leave it too long,' said the King. He gave a small sigh. 'I miss my dear Mary every day.' He fixed Henry with a thoughtful gaze. 'Of course, there will be a considerable fine to pay.'

'Of course, sire,' said Henry, inclining his head. He glanced sideways at Cate, his eyes shining.

* * *

As soon as they left St James's, Henry hailed a hackney carriage. He called up to the driver an address in the Strand and assisted Cate into the carriage. He jumped in after her and on the worn leather seat drew her close.

She rested her head against his chest and sighed. 'You are pardoned?' 'Yes, but there is one matter still to be deal with — why my name was on your father's lips.' She pulled back to stare up at the face she loved. 'I no longer care, Henry.'

'But I do, my love. We must find out, Cate, or this will lie between us for the rest of our lives.'

'What do you suggest?'

'We will take my coach to my estate at Melbury. My man of business may know something.'

'Yes,' she said in a dull voice. She knew he was right, but — oh — what if they learned something that might destroy them?

'It is a long journey,' he said, 'so tonight we stay at my London house.'

The carriage bumped over the ruts in the road, until the sound of Henry's voice cleared the fog of her thoughts.

'Here we are.'

She peered through the hackney's window and saw they had pulled up in front of a smart, stone-built house.

'Soon, Cate, all uncertainty will be over.'

Yes, she thought, and felt her heart shift with misgiving.

When they entered the house, the steward approached Henry and informed him that his man of business had arrived a short while ago.

'Excellent,' said Henry. 'That will save us a journey. I will see him now. Please serve Miss Trelawny tea in the drawing room.' He turned to Cate. 'I will not be long, my love.'

★ ★ ★

Cate was sipping tea nervously when Henry burst in and threw himself into the chair opposite.

'It seems that a contract was made some years ago between my father and yours.' He watched her face closely.

'In connection with some business interests?' she said, pouring another cup of tea.

'No,' said Henry, with a smile, taking the cup from her. 'In connection with their personal interests. You remember the meeting which took place at my father's house in Dorchester, when you and your father visited?'

She nodded, bewildered.

He spoke in a voice of amazement. 'It was to agree to a betrothal between us!'

Her pulse quickened. 'What do you mean?'

'We are betrothed.' His blue eyes sparkled.

Her tea cup fell to the floor. She stared at him.

'You and I?'

He laughed. 'Yes! We have been contracted to marry since that meeting, twelve years ago. What do you think of that?'

A glow spread through her body and she could not speak.

'It's been a long engagement.' He stepped quickly to her side and pulled her up, his arm circling her waist. 'I think we should remedy the matter as soon as we are able.'

'No.' She could barely focus on his words.

'No?' he said, frowning and drawing back.

'I mean,' she murmured, 'my father never told me about our betrothal.'

'But I think he did,' said Henry.

'No, my love. I am sure I would have remembered if he had.'

'Cate, I believe he was trying to tell you this when he said my name.'

Her cheeks grew pink. Could it be that her father wanted her to marry Henry and that he always had? As the Spanish Princess raced home with him, mortally wounded, he'd not wanted anyone but himself to tell her of the betrothal.

'It seems our respective fathers intended to tell us when I reached one and twenty,' said Henry. 'Alas, your mother passed away. Then, before I became of age, my own father died.'

'And your man of business has just

now told you this?'

'Yes. When I told him I intended to marry Miss Catherina Trelawny, he was delighted, informing me that it was what my father had always intended.' Henry's eyes glittered.

'But why had he not told you of this contract before?'

'He was not instructed to do so, and he said he was of the opinion that a man should choose his own bride.'

'Did you reprimand him for showing a lack of respect?' she said, trying not to smile.

'On the contrary. I praised him for his foresight. Of course a man should choose his own bride.' He caught her close again and smiled down into her eyes.

'As a woman should be free to choose her own husband,' said Cate.

Henry smiled and nodded. 'My love,' he said, in a low voice that sent her senses reeling. He lifted a hand and stroked her cheek, damp with hot tears. She tilted her chin up and he lowered his lips to hers.

She knew their days on the high seas

were over. There would always be pirate ships sailing on the far horizon and swords glinting under the sun, but it would happen elsewhere.

As if reading her mind, Henry said, 'Shall we make our home, have babies and grow content? As the years go by, we can tell our children and their children of battles and shipwrecks and pirates. I expect they will love our stories, as all children do, but I doubt they will believe them.'

'We will take our first born to meet Abella, sailing on the Spanish Princess as a merchant vessel with Mr Morgan the respectable captain,' she said, laughing joyously.

Henry smiled. 'And, who knows, perhaps one of our daughters or sons will grow up to become captain of their own ship one day.'

When it grew dark, Henry and Cate strolled in the walled garden in the warmth of the night. The moon was up, nearly full, and she fancied she could hear the low roar of the sea in the far distance. Cate stepped into Henry's arms and together they watched the moon rise over an ocean of stars.

We do hope that you have enjoyed reading this large print book.

Did you know that all of our titles are available for purchase?

We publish a wide range of high quality large print books including:
Romances, Mysteries, Classics
General Fiction
Non Fiction and Westerns

Special interest titles available in large print are:
The Little Oxford Dictionary
Music Book, Song Book
Hymn Book, Service Book

Also available from us courtesy of Oxford University Press:
Young Readers' Dictionary
(large print edition)
Young Readers' Thesaurus
(large print edition)

For further information or a free brochure, please contact us at:
Ulverscroft Large Print Books Ltd.,
The Green, Bradgate Road, Anstey,
Leicester, LE7 7FU, England.
Tel: (00 44) **0116 236 4325**
Fax: (00 44) **0116 234 0205**

PROMISE OF SPRING

Beth Francis

After the breakdown of her relation-
ship with Justin, Amy moves out of
town to a small village. In her cosy
cottage, with her kind next-door
neighbour Meg, she's determined
to make a fresh start. But there are
complications in store. Though Amy
has sworn never to risk her heart
again, she finds her friendship with
Meg's great-nephew Mike deepening
into something more. Until Mike's
ex-girlfriend Emma reappears on the
scene — and so does Justin ...

DATE WITH DANGER

Jill Barry

Bonnie spends carefree summers in the Welsh seaside resort where her mother runs a guesthouse. But things will change after she meets Patrik, a young Hungarian funfair worker. Both she and her friend Kay find love in the heady whirl of the fair — and are also are fast learning how people they thought they knew can sometimes conceal secrets. As Patrik moonlights for one of her mother's friends, Bonnie fears that he may be heading into danger . . .

ROSE'S ALPINE ADVENTURE

Christina Garbutt

Rose is in need of excitement. Taking a leap of faith, she flies to the Alps to take up the position of personal assistant to Olympic ski champion Liam Woods. Though she's never skied before — or even spent much time around snow — that's not going to stop her! But she hadn't bargained on someone trying to sabotage Liam's new venture ... or on her attraction to him. Can she and Liam save his business — and will he fall for her too?